TRUEFLAME

Fireborn Series Book Two

Vanessa Ricci-Thode

Thodestool Fiction

Publisher: Vanessa Ricci-Thode
Editors: Kristopher Mielke, Una Verdandi
Cover Designed by GetCovers

Library and Archives Canada Cataloguing in Publication

Print ISBN 978-1-7388450-2-6
Ebook ISBN 978-1-7388450-3-3

www.thodestool.ca

This is a first edition of *Trueflame*.

To my first audience:
Aimee, Mellyssa, Olivia and Stef

AUTHOR'S NOTE

Hello reader! This is the second book of the Fireborn series. If you're skipping book one or it's been a while, below is a spoiler-filled synopsis to get you caught up or to act as a refresher! Also note that Canadian spelling is being used throughout the book.

Previously in the Fireborn Series

Dionelle was born immune to fire. After moving to her new husband's farm, she catches the attention of the ruling nobles in the city. Forced into the position of dragon whisperer by the cruel Lord Draxli and Lady Karth Dunham, Dionelle is torn between keeping the peace in her kingdom and keeping her husband, Reiser's, desire to keep her safe from controlling her. Tension mounts between the newlyweds as Dionelle grows to love her job and the dragons she works with, exacerbated by her sister's jealous rage.

Then Dionelle fails to come home from her final apprenticing lesson. Discovering her mentor has been murdered, Reiser is pulled into the mystery of her disappearance and the snare of politics surrounding Pasdale's corrupt ruling nobles.

Reiser has no choice but to work with the dragons to find his wife, going against the Dunhams' wishes as they try to write Dionelle off for dead so they can select a new dragon whisperer. The dragons, however, will not be lied to—particularly the black dragoness who leads the local blaze and has grown fond of Dionelle. Enlisting Dionelle's best friend, a dragon scholar named Ondias, and finding allyship from two court wizards, Zev and Nandara, Reiser discovers that Dionelle's sister has manipulated a powerful wizard into murdering her mentor and banishing Dionelle to the fire realm. Dionelle's unique pyromantic nature is due to being part fire demon, allowing her to survive the fire realm. Taken by fire demons, Dionelle is trapped in their realm behind a wall of deceit exploiting the troubles in her life.

Meanwhile, the presence of a human in the fire realm is throwing all of the elements off balance, and the world is slowly tearing itself apart with wild weather swings and dangerous earthquakes.

In a desperate bid to save Dionelle and the world, Reiser becomes the first human to visit the dragon city—a towering structure of diamond and obsidian suspended over a valley—where he is enchanted to be fireproof and sent to the fire realm. He discovers Dionelle is alive and well—and pregnant. He uses the tenuous bond the pair forged before their separation to bring her home again. The elements stabilize, and Dionelle and Ondias are treated with a trip to the dragon city when Reiser is brought back there to remove the enchantment.

The story ends with the Dunhams removed from power: Draxli exiled and Karth executed. Dionelle's sister is imprisoned in a distant sanitorium. The king's cousin, Lady Zyx, is installed as the new ruler of Pasdale and peace returns to the land.

Trueflame content warnings: birth, burns, coma (magical), death by dragon, death by drowning, death by fire, demon possession, family estrangement, patriarchy, pregnancy in danger, sibling rivalry

Heat level: low

PROLOGUE

T he front door clattered open, jolting Dionelle from the edge of sleep, and the fire in the hearth flared as she sat alert. Neesha spilled drunkenly across the threshold, bringing the early winter chill with her. Dionelle let the fire dwindle back to embers, but one look at her daughter had the firelight rising, even as Dionelle closed her eyes and took a slow breath.

Neesha's rumpled clothes and the bits of straw in her tousled hair told Dionelle that the high colour on the girl's cheeks wasn't from drink alone.

Woman, Dionelle reminded herself. No matter how Neesha chose to act, she was nearly a woman.

"Ugh, Mamma, why do you bother waiting up?"

Dionelle had to wonder.

"It certainly isn't because I enjoy it. You've got lessons in the morning." Dionelle struggled to keep the accusation out of her tone. "Nandara expects you to be ready."

"I'll be ready. And on time," Neesha snapped.

"You're falling behind. Don't think Nandara doesn't tell me."

Neesha pinned Dionelle with that fiery gaze of hers, amber flashing over blue. She had roughly the same build as Dionelle, along with the similar amber-blue eyes, and startling white hair and skin like Dionelle once had, before the fire realm changed everything.

"I'll catch up." Neesha turned dismissively to pick bits of straw from her frizzy cumulus of bone-white hair, discarding the bits on the floor. It was always hard to tell if Neesha's actions were malicious or merely thoughtless.

But it certainly wouldn't be the girl sweeping the stones later. Dionelle suppressed a sigh.

"Catch up? Just like that? Oh, well, that's fine then." Dionelle pinched her mouth shut. She really did need to stop waiting up like this, letting the exhaustion get the better of her. But when else could she corner the girl and get her to talk?

Neesha glared, her eyes mirroring the rising firelight.

Dionelle held out a hand.

"Peace, girl. I trust Nandara not to let you take the Guild entrance exam before you're ready."

Neesha snorted. "I know better than to try. But I'll be ready when I'm eighteen, just you watch. I don't know why you think it will be so hard."

Dionelle couldn't help rolling her eyes; she *had* been through the exam herself. Did she really have to state the obvious?

"No one disputes your power or your capabilities," Dionelle said. "Only your wisdom."

"Ah, this again." Neesha scoffed and brushed passed Dionelle.

"Yes, this again." Dionelle let the fire flare behind her, halting Neesha. "Pasdale needs power like yours. I would welcome being able to properly work with you, to see you as a full-fledged wizard within the year."

"So that I can inherit your bloody dragons."

"Those *bloody dragons* have loved you like one of their own since your birth."

Neesha snorted derisively. "Only because I'm a bigger freak than you ever were."

Neesha's angry words always resurrected the spectre of Vyranna's cruelty. Dionelle advanced toward her daughter, not letting her retreat up the stairs to her room. Why couldn't she see?

"Nee, this isn't about the dragons. It's not about you being fireborn. Hard times are coming and—"

"No. *You're* the court's dragon whisperer, not me. Your hard times are your own." Neesha turned for the stairs.

Dionelle gripped her arm and held her daughter firm. Their eyes locked, flickering with firelight as the flames in the hearth flared. This close, Neesha's breath was thick with the smell of ale. Anger radiated from her. Dionelle pushed the fire all the way back down to embers, the girl's emotions and delusions of grandeur be damned. There was a reason Dionelle was a Guild wizard and Neesha was not.

Neesha pressed her mouth into a thin line.

"Tonight, you listen." Dionelle extinguished the embers, plunging the room into darkness despite Neesha's attempts to fan the flames. "There are troubles coming—rumours from the far north that dragons carry on the wind—but they are going to affect us all. I don't care if you become a whisperer or if you never marry or if you never finish your apprenticeship. I want you to be happy—"

"I'm perfectly happy when you leave me well enough alone!" Neesha ripped free of Dionelle's grip, the fire flaring once more.

"But you're not! Do you really think I can't see it? You're miserable and so you try to drown it in drink and bury it beneath an endless parade of lovers."

Dionelle closed her eyes against the past, but the spectre of her sister, Vyranna, rose up anyway. No one had understood Vyranna's pain, and she'd carried on then as Neesha did now until their mother, Sharice, had driven her from the house. And though Vyranna's actions perpetuated her own misery, she had struck out against Dionelle, blaming her. She'd betrayed the family and the kingdom, had nearly killed Dionelle in the process, nearly destroyed the world. For her efforts, she'd died alone in a cell not long after Neesha was born.

"You don't know anything!" Neesha hissed.

When Dionelle opened her eyes, the anger was gone, grim despair pulling on her limbs instead. Dionelle was failing to reach her wayward daughter just as she'd failed to reach her sister. She feared it would end with similar results. The saving grace was that whatever madness had lived in Vyranna's heart didn't appear to have touched Neesha. The girl was spiteful but she lacked Vyranna's hatred and cruelty.

"Fine. Drink yourself into a stupor and bed all the men and women that suit your fancy, if that's what truly makes you happy. You need to understand that it affects not just your family but the very kingdom."

"Oh, so your shame is a blight on the entire kingdom, is it? Maybe I'll bed someone in the middle of the market next time!"

The futility of it all pressed down on Dionelle and she sighed. It was so tempting to turn her back and let the fool of a girl do what she pleased. But

Neesha's actions hurt far more than her family. Those alleged dragon raids to the northeast didn't help worth a damn either.

"Nee, please. This isn't about what I think of what you do. It's gone beyond that. I pity you the attention you receive solely because of who your mother is. There's nothing fair about that. But I have as much duty to this kingdom and to peace as I do to my family. The kingdom's woes are our woes, after all. But powerful people have begun to take notice of your actions—people I need to be in favour with if I'm to continue to mediate and to serve both the king's people and the dragons."

"Oh, so Bly has stopped running to you with all the gossip, has he? Going straight to the top. Good for him. Good to have ambition."

Dionelle felt like she might sag right down into the floor. Neesha was all bitter resentment, rife with sarcasm, and lacking all reason. She heard what she wanted. It was like Neesha's whole world had boiled down to sibling rivalry with Bly. Dionelle didn't want to play this foolish game, but needed to talk Neesha around to the heart of the matter.

"He tells only me what he hears," Dionelle said softly. "He hasn't even uttered a word to your father."

Neesha shifted uncomfortably. At least the girl still deeply respected her father, and Dionelle knew she would be horrified if Reiser discovered even half of what Bly reported to her. She hoped the day would never come when she would have to use that against her daughter.

"What I do doesn't matter! Why can't you leave me alone?"

"It shouldn't matter, but it does. There are people at court, people who have Lady Zyx's ear, who say that if I can't manage my own family, what business do I have managing dragons."

"That's your problem! Stop trying to make it mine."

"If I lose my job, it's going to be this entire family's problem." Dionelle rubbed her hands across her face and stared at the stone floor between her and Neesha. "I know that sometimes the world's expectations can be stifling. You don't really have to meet those expectations, you know. You can make a show of it. If you accept a suitor or—"

Neesha growled in frustration and Dionelle forged ahead before she went off on another anti-suitor rant.

"You can always break a betrothal, but please consider at least accepting one for now."

"That's ridiculous!"

"Yes, it is. But this is the world we live in." Dionelle sighed. "Listen, Neesha, I don't care if you never work with dragons or wield a single fire spell in your entire life, but I need you to at least appear responsible so I can keep making those fools in the court listen to me before they start a dragon war."

But Dionelle saw from the set of Neesha's jaw and the way her mouth pressed into a thin line that she wasn't hearing any of it.

"Dragons are your problem."

"Please, Nee, focus on your studies and search your heart for what you truly want. I fear your selfishness is going to be our undoing."

As Neesha bristled, the fire flared. Dionelle quelled it with a thought, like pinching a candle flame between fingertips, and wished her daughter was half so easy to deal with. Neesha turned in a huff and disappeared up the stairs, leaving Dionelle in a pool of darkness.

CHAPTER ONE

Neesha dragged her weary body up the laneway toward the pair of homes, casting a forlorn glance at the stone house she was no longer welcome in before setting her jaw and angling for the older wooden house she shared with her grandmother. She heard giggles and shouts and spotted her brothers horsing around on the front porch.

The sight always brought a smile to her face.

But if they were out there goofing off, it had to be lunchtime already. Neesha frowned up at the overcast sky, spring rains looming, hiding the time of day from her. How had the entire morning passed? Everything seemed to take longer these days. She scowled.

Four months of brain-fog. Four months of everything taking twice as long—including those lessons she swore she'd get caught up on. She was farther behind, even though she largely did as her mother wished and stayed home to study and rest. Not that there was much choice in the matter.

Word got around.

"Give it or I'll just start chewing on you!" Breen's indignant voice cut through Neesha's foul thoughts. Her youngest brother was currently trying to snatch the plate Bly held high above the younger boy's head. Bly had him by the shoulder to keep him away.

Neesha smiled and shook her head.

"Never ends with you two," she called.

Distracted, Bly grinned over at her and Breen seized the opportunity, tilting his head to chomp down on Bly's fingers. The older boy screamed, his voice cracking as it so often did these days. Neesha laughed as Breen reclaimed his lunch.

"Really now, Bly, haven't you got anyone else to pick on?" Neesha joined them.

"Eh, there's only you. You don't give me much to work with anymore. Not without all your evening activities."

Everything had been in jest until that last jibe, all hard edges and dark. Breen's grin vanished as quickly as Neesha's scowl reappeared.

"Come on, Bly, that wasn't fair." Breen edged closer, almost between the two.

"Nothing she's done is fair for any of us," Bly snapped. It was clear from the way he kept glaring at Neesha, that his words were directed at her as much as a response to Breen.

"I've done nothing to you." Neesha's throat tightened with anger. "Stop being such a godsdamned child."

"Nee, of the three of us, you're the one with the most growing up to do. And soon." He glanced at her stomach with that last comment.

Neesha wondered if she could scowl harder without hurting herself.

"Come on, don't fight," Breen pleaded. "It's lunchtime. Don't listen to him, Nee, he just needs to eat."

Bly pushed the boy off. "If she doesn't need to grow up, what's Mamma got Stone here for?"

When Neesha's expression fell, Bly grinned triumphantly, though it looked more like a sneer.

"Blasted moons, not this again," Neesha muttered, pushing past her brothers and into the modest farmhouse she shared with Nanny Sharice.

There was no sign of Nanny anywhere. But Neesha spotted Stone's large bulk at their kitchen table, his dark gaze drawn to her as she came in. He didn't move otherwise, kept his hands folded on the tabletop, the perpetual dirt stains under his nails resulting from his day's labour were a touch darker than his skin. Her mother's narrow frame stood next to him, always an interesting contrast with her pale skin and white-streaked auburn hair. She also looked up as Neesha came in.

It was Dionelle's presence that shocked Neesha the most. It was such a rarity these days for the woman to be home while the sun still shone. Home and not surrounded by dragons. She was usually in the courts, serving as negotiator, as dragon whisperer, between Pasdale's nobility and its blaze of dragons.

Dionelle smiled warmly and Neesha's guard instantly went up.

"Ah, here you are. I was beginning to wonder if we'd have to fetch you from Nandara's."

"Oh, that'd be a sight," Neesha said, her tone low and frosty. "And the last thing I need."

Neesha glanced at Stone, acknowledging his presence, and then went into the kitchen, her back to them both, so she could get some lunch. She hadn't heard her mother's pursuit, but Dionelle's voice came from behind her.

"Nee, please show some respect for our guest."

"He's *your* guest. I haven't time for manners."

"Well that's nothing new. And it's a wonder Stone still has any interest in you, especially now."

"I don't need anyone's interest." Neesha glared at her mother, but it was Stone she saw, sitting quietly behind Dionelle. He had that same earnest expression despite Neesha's rude barbs, and she turned away, feeling like she'd kicked a puppy.

"Someone's got to support you," Dionelle said, her words clipped. "And don't you dare feed me your foolish lines about how you'll do it all yourself. Maybe you had a hope of it if you'd made entrance to the Guild by now, but Nandara has told me of your progress. Or lack of it. Tell me, Nee, how are you going to manage it all without work? Are you learning to conjure money then?"

"I'll get caught up and get into the Guild before my birthday. Plenty of time."

Neesha kept her back to her mother and Stone, busy trying to assemble a sandwich with hands that trembled with rage, but there was pity in Dionelle's voice when she spoke.

"Please, Nee, you're not fooling anyone except yourself. You've thrown yourself headlong into your apprenticeship these last months and still you are behind. Take the match with Stone. Take the stability that comes with it, the security of having somewhere to live past the autumn and someone to support you until you have the Guild's backing to support yourself."

"Oh yes? You think that's what will happen?" Neesha spun around, livid, holding her mother's gaze and refusing to notice Stone. "Once you've forced me into being his wife, that'll be the end of it. No need for the Guild then, so why bother?"

But the pity in Dionelle's expression only deepened.

"Is that why you resist so hard? You think marriage, or even motherhood, means an end to your dreams? Do you really think you have to be outside of any community in order to be fully independent? Neesha, honestly! Look at me—am I married? And a mother? Am I also doing what I love?"

"Oh, and because settling for a farmer worked out just fine for you, I've got to do the same?"

Dionelle glanced down at Neesha's stomach, and Neesha resisted the urge to fold her arms over it. Refused to hide, even if there wasn't anything to hide. Not yet. Though it wore on her how no one would come out and say what the real issue was—the real reason she was being rushed to accept a suitor, that anyone still interested would do. The agreement for the family to remain silent had been reached immediately and unanimously the moment Neesha's *condition* had been one she couldn't hide from her father any longer.

"Your circumstance, by your own doing, is far different than mine ever was." Dionelle's voice was low, carrying a note of threat to it. "Stone's continued interest is a blessing, Neesha. It's the best you're going to get."

"I don't need it."

"Just talk to him before you decide that." Dionelle gestured to an empty seat at the table.

Neesha shook her head and stared at the scuffed wood of the table that had been there since long before her mother had even been born. This was the third time Stone had been to their house to discuss the possibility of marrying Neesha. The first had been a year ago, back when her father had still been speaking to her. Before she'd ruined it all, they'd tried other desperate attempts to find her a husband—a whole parade of snobby sons of courtiers out to claim her like some sort of carnival prize, wed the pretty daughter of the famous dragon whisperer—never listening to what Neesha wanted.

They didn't believe she could do it on her own.

With the snobby courtiers too good for Neesha now, her family kept trying to encourage a union with Stone, a man ten years her senior. A widower with two small children, River and Ember, and some of Pasdale's best farmland. Neesha looked into Stone's wide, smiling face and lost her nerve.

"You know it would be just like this." Stone gestured around them. "Peace and quiet, farmwork if you want it. Near enough to the courts if you want that."

"Yes, the courts are what I want. Being a court wizard is *all* I want. Thank you for your interest, Stone, but I'll not be your wife."

He didn't move but somehow grew smaller. He held her gaze, but his dark eyes no longer had the same light to them. Neesha tried not to be angry with him, this was all her mother's doing, but the silent way he took her abuse—it was so cowardly! Maybe she'd put a moment's consideration into the proposal if he'd show some strength. But they should all know better.

"I'm sorry, Stone. It's not you. I'll not be *anyone's* wife." She glared at her mother. "I don't know why you think my answer is going to change."

"Do you really not?" Dionelle asked, her tone sharp.

"I have months to finish my apprenticeship. I don't have time for this." Neesha stacked her lunch plate on top of the books she'd left on the table and scooped it all up, not looking back as she marched up the stairs to her room.

She would be eighteen at summer's end and then the autumn would bring drastic changes. It was when her midwife insisted the baby they all refused to speak of would arrive. Her family promised there would no longer be a place for her, even in this house with her grandmother, once she was an adult. Neesha hoped they were wrong, that their anger would fade with the seasons, but she'd be ready all the same. She'd push through the exhaustion and finish her apprenticeship. She'd damn-well take care of herself—of both of them. She was too close to fail now.

CHAPTER TWO

L ord Draxli Dunham lounged in a tall-back chair, the closest thing to a throne he had since his days in Pasdale, and gazed over the rail of the terrace to the village below. He took a weary look around at the plain stone, simple wood and rickety furniture of his shabby surroundings, longing for marble, wrought iron, finely crafted gold leafing. His chair was the only piece of furniture out on the otherwise empty terrace that wasn't rickety. He snorted and looked out over the valley, verdant despite the season, and he smiled inwardly. That, at least, was going well, even if he couldn't yet afford to build a proper estate on the mountainside. He was lucky enough to have a home with a roof made of something other than thatch out in these forsaken backwaters.

"But that was the point, wasn't it, Uncle?"

Thinking of his uncle, the king, stung him, and he absently pulled out the pocketwatch where he kept the small image of his Lady Karth. The watch had been a mere trifle when she'd thoughtlessly given it to him on a whim so many years ago, but it was one of the few treasures he had left. Even such a common trinket was a luxury in this cursed place. It helped lend him the air of power he needed if he was to avenge her.

He gave her image a final glance, savouring the confident line of her jaw and her alluring gaze, as if she would devour the artist whole—she likely had meant to. He smiled, but there was no joy in it. She was long dead and if not for this remnant of their life together, she would have faded to little more than a gaping wound in his life.

He cherished the memories. They had driven him this far, and they would drive him farther still. He would reclaim his rightful place at Pasdale's helm. He had supporters there yet, still loyal and doing his bidding. Sending him information. But there was much work to do if he hoped to unseat his accusers and restore his good name.

Draxli snapped the watch shut and dropped it back into his pocket, leaning over the railing to observe his pitiful realm below. A scruffy kingdom for a now-scruffy lord. Draxli's light brown hair always seemed in need of a trim these days. At least the way it was peppered with grey lent him an added air of dignity and authority. It was excellent counterbalance to his sun-wizened skin, hardened from years of toiling in the muck. Getting himself dirty like a peasant, of all the ungodly things.

But that would change. It was already changing. He smiled down at his hands, roughly manicured but scrubbed clean. All traces of dirt long forgotten.

He did not turn when his servant tapped at the terrace door before opening it.

"M'lord? He has arrived."

"Bring him."

He heard the servant's feet shuffling back into the manor without closing the door, and a few moments later the sound of footsteps returned. At that, Draxli stood and turned in one swift motion. The smile that never quite reached his pale blue eyes burst across his features—not too wide, he hoped. He was never quite certain exactly how many teeth to show. Not that it really mattered.

He warmly greeted the young aquamancer escorted by the servant, gripping his hands—but not *too hard*—in a welcoming handshake.

Calling him a young man was a stretch. The wizard before him was little more than a boy. And a fool, no doubt, if he'd tried for his Guild entrance so early. The boy was lanky and tall, taller than Draxli, but probably half Draxli's bulk, with a shy smile and shaggy blond hair. A wee lamb ripe for the taking. Draxli's grin widened and the boy before him stilled.

"You know why you're here?" Draxli asked.

"Yes, m'lord."

"Show me."

The boy nodded and seemed to grow larger, inflating before Draxli's eyes. His nervous, roving gaze focused as his bushy brows furrowed in concentration, and the boy's lips pressed into a bloodless line. He raised his arms and then brought his hands together, the space between them thickening as he pulled moisture out of the very air, leaving Draxli's skin feeling tight—almost sunburned—from the sudden dryness around him. The boy kept going until he commanded a puddle large enough to fill a mop bucket. It rolled over itself, tumbling like a stationary river between the boy's hands.

Genuinely delighted now, Draxli thought his grin would split his face in half, his dry lips ready to crack. And he knew the boy wasn't done yet.

With the water called up before him, the boy chanted, murmuring softly so that Draxli couldn't make out his words. The water became a vicious whirlpool, and a thin line of mist, like smoke come alive, rose from its centre. The mist formed a mass in the air between Draxli and the boy, slowly taking shape, elongating with a watery shimmer until it was almost as tall as Draxli. Then it emitted a sound like rain hitting the leaves of a great forest, whispering to him at the edge of understanding.

"It's speaking," Draxli said calmly, not wanting to let on too much. Not yet.

"It wants to know why we've called it here," the boy answered nervously.

"And do you know why?"

The boy nodded grimly and moved to the edge of the terrace, taking the water demon with him. He spoke to it, and Draxli was surprised to hear that same rainwater sound coming from the boy. Thankfully the boy had his back to him. Draxli composed himself immediately and joined the boy at the railing, watching as the swirling vortex grew into a rushing torrent, pouring over the railing and hurtling down the mountainside to the dry river basin below. The water seemed endless, roaring like no dragon ever could, as it burst forth from the place where the boy held a demon between his hands.

"Well done." Draxli allowed a touch of approval into his tone, signalling that the boy could stop.

With a whisper of rain, the boy coaxed the demon back into the vortex, the torrent ebbing away to mist and then a memory. The demon disappeared into the puddle and the puddle rapidly evaporated back into the air. It was easier to breathe, and the inside of Draxli's mouth no longer felt parched. The boy turned shyly back to Draxli, unable to meet the man's gaze, his face full of fear and hope. It was a shame that the Wizards Guild had let such talent slip from them on a ridiculous formality, but it would be his gain.

The other aquamancers Draxli had already gathered to this once drought-stricken nation left quite the impression. He had done well with the timing, his other allies having driven away the region's dragons as the first aquamancers arrived. This little backwater of bumpkins wasn't *that* slow, and Draxli's whispered intimations that the dragons were a drain on resources were enough to get the rumours flowing. The villagers had come up with the rest.

Now the belief was widespread that the fires of the dragons had sucked the very moisture from the air. That the dragons caused the drought. Draxli's aquamancers were subtle but quick in restoring crops, cementing beliefs. Trade routes had reopened, now that there was something more than dust to trade, and the rumours accompanied the farmers' wares. Draxli sent them southward to Pasdale.

Soon.

Draxli would certainly need the boy if the next stage of his plan was to succeed.

"Well done, indeed," Draxli crooned. "Those old fools will one day know the grave error they made when they turned away such magnificent power."

The boy's blue eyes shone with barely-suppressed tears and Draxli smiled internally.

"I have been searching a decade for your kind of talent. You are a rare find indeed, and I will not make the same error the Guild did."

For now, this approval seemed to be all the boy needed, though Draxli would suss out the rest of the boy's needs before he ever drew upon them. The boy seemed simple enough, but it would take time to learn his heart—did he simply seek vindication, or would he demand revenge and great power as well? Draxli would need to tread carefully until he was certain.

"What is your name, boy?" Draxli asked gently.

"Loch."

Draxli quirked an eyebrow at the coincidence.

"My mother's family is aquamancers for generations back."

"Ah, so you have family prestige behind you as well. Very good." He paused a moment, considering. He turned to the servant. "Prepare the announcement for the village. Let them know where this truly blessed gift of water came from in these parched times."

The servant bowed, knowing well enough when he'd been dismissed and motioned for Loch that it was time to go.

"Thank you, Lord Dunham." Loch bowed gratefully. "I won't let you down, sir."

Draxli smiled at his retreating back, relishing the new lordship he had regained. It had been many a long year since he had enjoyed the privileges it afforded him. He had once lived nearly as well as his Lord Uncle, King of Golden Hill. For years since his exile, Draxli had feared he would never know prosperity again. But just as one stubborn farmer and his meddling wife had undone it all, this new valley full of simple folk offered him hope. It had not been an easy battle, but it would prove worthwhile when he reclaimed what was his. Once the servant and Loch were gone, he pulled the watch out and smiled down at his lady love.

"Soon, my dear. My darling Karth. They will know my loss. I will avenge you."

CHAPTER THREE

Neesha listlessly poked her fork around on her plate. Nanny Sharice had gone to the trouble of preparing Neesha's favourite meal, which only made Neesha feel guilty that she couldn't enjoy it. But the baby seemed to be pressed right up against her chin these days, and half the time eating only added to her misery. She nibbled at a slice of rabbit and watched her gathered family members, trying to ignore the empty chair that should be filled by her mother.

Dionelle's absence was a mixed blessing. Neesha wanted the family to be together, for things to be like they had been only a few short seasons ago. There had been so much laughter, even if it was often threaded with tension. Now everyone was silent. Sombre. Uncle Cusec huddled at the far end of the table with his wife, Seina, and their two daughters, Cavvi and Serra who were younger than Breen. They whispered amongst themselves as they ate, theirs a completely different world, one far removed from the drama Neesha brought everywhere she went.

Uncle Cusec loved her, but the tension between her and her parents was too difficult for him—too much like how he'd grown up. Neesha had heard all the stories about her long-dead aunt, Vyranna, a terror consumed by madness after nearly starting a dragon war because of her jealousy.

Dionelle always compared Neesha to her aunt, always careful to stipulate that Neesha, at least, had her mind intact, but it always made Neesha furious. Her mother always had to compare her to someone else. Nothing Neesha did was her own. She was fireborn and powerful like her mother—but not exactly like her mother, she was far more powerful than

Dionelle had ever been—and white like a winter night, the way her mother apparently had been before leaving most of her power in the fire realm.

If Neesha wasn't being reminded about how she was powerful and strange like her mother, then it always came back to Vyranna. And Neesha couldn't help but wonder if maybe her aunt just hadn't been very good at managing reasonable anger at what society expected of women. Neesha let out a long weary breath and ran her hand across her vast belly as the baby did another flip. Well, that was a spell of trouble Aunt Vyranna had never gotten into. Impending motherhood—unwed, at that—was unique to Neesha in the family, though no one really seemed interested in addressing it.

Her mother's empty chair at what was supposed to be Neesha's birthday celebration was testament enough. Dionelle was ashamed of her, but mostly only cared about her duty and how Neesha's indiscretions were costing her.

"She can stuff her duty to the kingdom up a dragon's steaming backside," Neesha muttered bitterly. She glanced to her mother's empty chair and her scowl only deepened.

Never mind the way her father gobbled down his food without tasting it, as usual, desperate to put in his appearance and get back to the main house—away from her. His broad shoulders were tense and hunched, his olive complexion and brown eyes darker in the shadow of his windswept brown hair as he kept his focus on his food. She couldn't remember the last time he'd spoken a word to her, kind or otherwise.

Nanny Shar, at least, was ecstatic about her first grandbaby regardless of circumstances—her blue eyes sparkling and pink cheeks glowing any time the topic came up—and Neesha suspected it was the only reason she was allowed to live in the old homestead. As of today, Neesha was an adult and had fully expected to be turned out. It seemed she would be allowed to live with her grandmother at least until the baby arrived.

Neesha tried not to think about that, tried instead to find a strand of joy in the day. But there was the sudden scrape of wood on wood as Reiser shoved his chair away from the table and stood, his meal finished.

"Reiser, please," Sharice said. "I've got the pastries ready, just stay for those."

Neesha knew he wouldn't, and he didn't. Her father said nothing to her grandmother and only continued his way across the kitchen and out the back door, heading back to the large stone house that Neesha was no longer allowed in, and hadn't been since the day the swell of her stomach had become something she could no longer hide from her parents.

Her brothers would stay for the pastries and maybe they'd have some token gift for her—something trivial they'd made, or some small trinket from the market. The tension would ease and Uncle Cusec and his family would relax. Things would feel all right for a little while. They'd have the pastries, Nanny Shar would have presents and stories. The night would grow late and then Uncle Cusec would take his family home and Nanny would keep up with the stories and her optimistic spin about how everything would be just fine, until Neesha collapsed into bed from exhaustion.

At least she still had a bed. Nanny had been living in the old farmhouse since Uncle Cusec had moved to Pasdale when Neesha was barely old enough for school. Neesha didn't remember when the stone house behind the farmhouse had been built, and she didn't remember her family's move to it, or the days when they'd lived in the old farmhouse. But she was living here with Nanny, who still loved her as she had loved Vyranna who had been far worse.

Neesha toyed with her food, occasionally glancing at her mother's seat. Her mother's absence wore on her, of course, and while Dionelle insisted she had no choice—Lady Zyx was hosting the king and Dionelle just *had* to make them see the truth about the north—Neesha couldn't help but feel that it was a personal slight.

"Nee, dear, what did you learn with Nandara today?" Nanny Shar asked, the room brightening with the sound of her voice. She swept some of her greying auburn hair out of her face and rested her chin in her hand.

While most of Neesha's apprenticeship focused on studying for her Guild entrance exams, she had plenty to learn before she'd be ready for it. Neesha intended to gain Guild entry before she had her baby, but the timing would be close.

"Nandara's got me started on healing," Neesha said, grateful to have conversation, to pierce the silence left in her father's wake.

"Oh, now there's a practical skill," Nanny said, then went on to extol the virtues of a wizard who knew her way around healing spells. The work prospects were endless for a healer.

Uncle Cusec nodded along with Sharice's speech, but Neesha just smiled. With only one day of lessons on the subject, Neesha didn't know yet if she had any proficiency as a healer. She hadn't tried healing so much as a papercut yet. That was a few lessons away.

While they spoke of her apprenticeship, Nanny brought out the tray of pastries. The rest of the family presented Neesha with her gifts.

Bly was nearly done school and Dionelle had found him work as a scribe, so this year's gifts were more extravagant than Neesha was used to. He presented her with comfortable new boots and a new riding cloak, both things she was in dire need of. Breen worked the fields and also had more to spend on his sister, gifting her with a dazzling pendant that brought out the radiance of her amber-blue eyes.

Neesha couldn't help think of the similar pendant her mother wore, one she'd had since marrying Reiser. That one was a rich, dark blue, swirling with silver light. That was a love stone, a rare gem, even rarer to be filled with love's light as it was. Neesha didn't know much about precious stones, but doubted her brother could afford something like that.

"Stone helped him pick it out," Bly said with a wink. "That man's a gem, Nee."

Neesha rolled her eyes and accepted the gifts without taking the bait. While she appreciated that Bly had stopped his childish tattling, his efforts to vicariously ingratiate Stone with her was just as irritating. The boy was not subtle in his intentions. Take the match, get married, stop embarrassing us all.

"Oh shut it, Bly," Breen said. "No one needs to hear about that tonight. Have another pastry."

Neesha smirked, although she knew the boys were bullied at school over her indiscretions, and that was something she wished she could take back. But it was done. At least their betrothals were no longer in jeopardy, though Neesha didn't know what her mother had done to change that.

Breen nudged her and she found another package in amongst all the wrapping. It was a cloth doll.

"For the baby." He stared at his plate, knowing they weren't supposed to talk about it, but not seeming to care. She had nearly forgotten how endearing the boys could be when out of the presence of their parents.

Nanny had already presented her gift that morning, an heirloom quilt that had been her grandmother's. One of them had gone to Dionelle and Reiser after they'd wed, and the other had been meant for Vyranna.

Uncle Cusec and Aunt Seina had brought her books, as they always did. One was on dragon lore—though Neesha had little interest in the beasts—one a book of spells, and two were books of fairy stories, one of them a refurbished copy of the one Cusec had shared with his sisters when they'd been children. Another gift as much for the baby as Neesha. Even with the child expected before the end of the next moon, she hadn't anticipated receiving so much for the babe. Her family had been doing such a good job at pretending the indiscretion had never happened that Neesha had half expected them to go right on ignoring the child for the rest of its life.

"Thank you." Neesha tried to be sincere. She would need almost everything they'd given her, and Breen's gift of the necklace showed a certain thoughtfulness Neesha hadn't expected out of the boy.

Of course, just as her mother continued to think her a girl—even now that she was eighteen and nearly a mother herself—Neesha kept forgetting that her brothers were nearly men. Both had been long ago matched with daughters of wizards and courtiers, and Bly had begun a proper courtship with his betrothed.

Neesha sat back in her chair, watching her family dig into the desserts and waiting for the chatter to resume. The tension had melted out of the air, and Neesha grinned to herself about the promise the night held.

But then the back door creaked open and clattered shut, and Neesha was dismayed to see her mother enter the kitchen. Neesha tried to keep calm, but the lamps had all flared with her sudden burst of emotion while everyone else acted as though they hadn't seen a thing.

"Happy birthday, my darling." Dionelle leaned over the chair to give Neesha a quick, one-armed hug and then set a package down in front of her.

"This one's from me and Nandara both," she said. "Part birthday present and part Guild entrance gift."

"I haven't taken my exams yet."

"You don't plan on passing them?" Dionelle's tone was playful, certain in Neesha's abilities as a wizard, but Neesha read some of the distrust that bred the comment. She knew her mother half expected her to throw her exams, just to be contrary. As much as Neesha wanted to, wizardry was the only thing that really gave her purpose. Dragon whispering had been her mother's calling, and working magic was Neesha's.

"You'd like that, wouldn't you?" Neesha said. "One more sob story for you to share at the market."

Dionelle recoiled, frowning, but it wasn't anger that Neesha saw in her mother's expression. It was sadness. And disappointment, but Neesha was used to seeing that. Dionelle pressed her lips together—Neesha saw Dionelle weighing her reaction and saw everyone else watching from her periphery.

"Open it," Dionelle said, her tone light, tinged with excitement despite Neesha's abrasive comment.

Neesha sized her up for a moment, trying to decide what game her mother was having, then pulled back the crinkled paper. She froze, shocked and delighted, when she saw the amethyst fabric, a whole pile of it. She picked it up, the softest thing she'd ever felt, giving it a shake to drape it across her lap. It was dragon skin. And if it was coming from her mother, it was sanctioned—possibly even from a dragon Dionelle had once known.

"Mamma, this is beautiful," Neesha gasped, feeling a moment of guilt for her comment earlier. Dragon skin wizarding robes. Neesha needed new ones, especially if she wanted to be presentable in the Guild once she was accepted, but dragon skin, and in her favourite colour no less, was far beyond anything she'd ever expected.

Neesha grew suspicious. Dragon skin was overkill, more than any wizard would ever need in daily spellcasting, or for anything ever. And dragon skin was fireproof. Her skin buzzed.

"Is this so I can start talking to your dragons?"

Dionelle blinked and tilted her head. "It's to keep your clothing protected, just as mine does."

Dionelle's firecloak was not made of dragon skin though, and had been enchanted by her mentor so many years before.

"Yes, it's fireproof. I remember that much about dragon skin. What do I need with a fireproof cloak if not to commune with dragons? And won't they be insulted to see me wearing their friend?"

Dionelle stood with her mouth opening and closing, not making a sound.

Uncle Cusec cut in. "It's a lovely gift, Neesha. It's such a great addition to the others from tonight. I hope you've had a good birthday, but we've got to head home."

His words rushed out, tumbling over each other; Aunt Seina was already gathering the girls into their riding cloaks and ushering them to the door. Bly and Breen each grabbed some more pastries from the tray and called their goodnights to her as they headed out the back door and back to the main house.

Just like that, it was all over. Only a few minutes of her mother's presence and the night's promise had been shattered. The room brightened as the lamps flared, and a tingle of rage tightened Neesha's chest.

"Nee, it's just a fireproof cloak. It doesn't mean anything. It was Nandara's idea, really. You're a pyromancer and you will be working with fire daily. Whether the fire comes from dragons or not isn't the concern. I just wanted you to have something you can use when you begin your practice."

The confusion was still in Dionelle's voice, as was the sadness and disappointment. Neesha thought she may have liked the gift if it hadn't driven away the family she'd so desperately wanted to spend the evening with. She was left to spend the evening in her mother's company. The only way it could get any worse was if her father were to return.

"Why did you have to come here?" Neesha asked.

"It's your birthday. I wanted to celebrate it with you... Why wouldn't I come?"

"You've done plenty good enough keeping away."

"Neesha, I couldn't very well turn down summons from the king." Dionelle shook her head. "I came home as soon as I could. They wanted me there longer, but I told them it was your birthday."

"I'm amazed they'd let you go just to celebrate with the pariah."

Dionelle looked desperately to Nanny, who stood next to the table shaking her head. Nanny stayed out of the argument, though. She always did.

"If you're going to read malice into my intentions and choose to be offended, then I can't stop you," Dionelle said. "You're an adult and your choices are your own. I hope the day comes soon that you remember the permanence of your actions."

She looked down at Neesha's large, round belly and then turned away. Neesha was surprised, Dionelle usually tried harder to defend her intentions against Neesha's anger. This was new.

"Do you really believe I don't see the permanence of this?" Neesha snapped, standing up and following her mother.

Dionelle paused and turned, but her expression told Neesha everything she needed to know.

"Even now, you see a girl before you. Don't you?"

"When you behave like this, what else am I supposed to see?"

"You really think I haven't noticed that all your attempts to match me have ended? You haven't even had Stone around! That you've been focused on supporting my work as a wizard. You know I'll have to support myself. I won't find a husband after this."

Dionelle sighed wearily, resigned. "Perhaps the baby's father—"

"No," Neesha snapped. "This isn't about him, it's never going to be about him. He's not the answer."

Neesha couldn't admit to her mother that she wasn't actually certain who the child's father was, that she hoped for an answer once her baby came into the world. She wouldn't tell Dionelle, even if she knew. If her suspicions were correct, though, her child's father was dead. Dionelle would try to press for a match with some other member of the man's family—a brother, a cousin, a widowed uncle. *Anyone* would do. Neesha didn't need to be matched. She didn't *want* to be matched. She'd find her own way or she wouldn't, and she didn't see why Dionelle couldn't understand that.

"What is the answer, then?" Dionelle said. "You are certainly not going to continue to live off the hard work of this family without contributing. Your grandmother won't be around forever to help you."

"Oh, you're just going to turn me out, are you? Because that worked so well for Auntie."

Neesha hadn't realized what she'd said until Nanny gasped. It was maybe not the best time to use her habitual term of endearment for a woman she'd never even met, but it always had the power to get a reaction out of her mother. A reaction from Nanny wasn't what she wanted. Neesha froze, her face dropping and she turned to her grandmother, but the woman had turned away from her and slowly made her way toward the stairs.

"Vyranna brought her own grief," Dionelle said, her tone low and threatening. "She did it just like this, too. When are you going to realize that you are the owner of your misery? We have done nothing but support you up until now, even when you reject us and abuse us at every turn. Even your wounded father still supports you through your apprenticeship and helps provide for you and your coming child. Neesha, we have done everything we can for you. If you do not want to suffer your aunt's fate, then you need to learn from her mistakes, and soon."

Dionelle turned and went to the back door, but she stopped for one final dig.

"I'm sorry your birthday had to end like this. Do what you want with the gift."

Dionelle's tone was strangely defeated, her posture sagged as she pushed out the back door and into the night. Neesha growled in wordless, clenched-fist frustration, the lamps and hearthfire flaring as she did. Hands still fisted, she looked out the back door to the stone house she was unwelcome in. Her father joined her mother in the front room, the pair of them silhouetted by gentle firelight. Dionelle slowly shaking her head as Reiser folded her into his embrace.

Neesha glared across the darkness at the love and trust she would never have. There wasn't a man in Pasdale, maybe even in all the world, who would love her the way her parents loved each other. And nights like this made her wonder if they spared any of their love for her.

There had been a woman Neesha had taken as a lover once who would have made a glorious partner. Yenette. Shy and sensitive, she'd brought out a gentle side Neesha hadn't known she had. Too bad that would go over even worse than remaining an unwed mother.

No. There was no one else Neesha could rely upon but herself.

Neesha looked around, her gifts scattered across the table, the uneaten pastries on the tray, and the room otherwise empty. She looked to the stairs where her grandmother had disappeared and she sat heavily in her seat, oblivious to the roaring flames around her.

Furious as the comparisons to her aunt made her, Neesha knew the truth in it. Knew she sat alone because of it. Just like her aunt, Neesha knew she'd have to survive on her own. There would be no legendary romance. Her family would not support her for long. So even as she shook with rage, she turned to her books of spellcraft.

CHAPTER FOUR

The words in Neesha's book blurred as her eyes unfocused. She blinked, scowled down at the pages. She was over a month behind in her studies, but within the week Nandara would decide when to put Neesha through her Guild entrance exams. Neesha had to be ready. Had to be. Sitting at the big study table in Nandara's workshop, she glared at the pages, brow furrowed. But the words got lost in the whispers across the room.

Nandara knelt on a mat in front of the hearth while a large, wavering flame hung in the air in front of her. A vaguely animal-like flame hissing and sparking in response to Nandara's whispers. Nandara remained focused, her pale brow furrowed in concentration, her green eyes focused on the demon.

Neesha needed to concentrate on healing theory, but how could she focus on anything at all when Nandara had a fire demon *right there*? Neesha should have mentioned how distracting it was the very first time Nandara had called one up while Neesha worked on other things. But then Nandara would stop doing it. Neesha couldn't help it. She *had* to see Nandara doing elemental magic like this.

She had no idea what Nandara did with the demons she called up. There were usually random objects on the floor in front of Nandara, like the glass bowl she had now. This was advanced magic. The sort of thing Neesha needed to be a Guild member in order to practice.

Neesha looked at the book in front of her and despaired that she was barely halfway through it. At the stack of books she had left to study before she could take her exam. Her mind was already bursting with knowledge. And yet for all of this study, she would gain little more than the basic requirements for Guild membership. To have any sort of rank within the Guild and actually practice advanced elemental magic the way Nandara did, Neesha would have to study years more.

Neesha shook her head and focused on the book. Healing was as fascinating as it was difficult. And when Nandara had let her seal up a minor wound, proving she could do it at all, Neesha had been riveted. But still, it couldn't pierce the siren song of elemental magic. Especially not when Nandara was half a room away practicing pyromancy. Advanced pyromancy.

Neesha could do advanced pyromancy in her sleep. She breathed pyromancy. She *was* pyromancy. That she shouldn't be doing half the things she did was of no concern to her. She couldn't help it. She'd been doing advanced pyromancy since she was a toddler. Her mother had been teaching her pyromancy since she was an infant, out of necessity to keep her and everyone around her safe. If Neesha could be judged on her elemental magic alone, she'd have been a Guild member years ago.

Sighing, Neesha put her finger under the line she was reading, forcing herself to pay attention. A glance at Nandara told her the woman was wrapping things up anyway. The demon shrank into the fire. Nandara set the bowl aside.

Neesha went back to reading about fractures. This particular book wasn't about spellcraft at all. It was a surgeon's book. But healing was healing, regardless of the method. She'd only gone a few more pages when Nandara's shadow fell over her.

"Well?"

"Fascinating stuff. Do you do much healing?" Neesha asked.

"I haven't the proficiency at it."

It wasn't only Nandara's friendship with Dionelle that had the woman as Neesha's mentor. They were well-matched in their skill sets. Nandara could perform the spells required of a Guild member, including some basic healing, but it was her elemental magic that made her a master wizard. Nandara had nearly as much grasp of all four elements as Neesha had over fire alone.

Nandara held up a chicken bone between her forefingers and thumbs, snapping it and setting both pieces down in front of Neesha.

Ah, a test. Neesha grinned.

She worked the two pieces together, fitting them as closely as she could, then focused her spellwork on the break. A cold rush went through her body, the magic pulling from her as the seam blurred and came together. Lips pressed together and brows furrowed, a headache throbbed behind her eyes the harder she concentrated. Despite the lightheadedness, Neesha broke out into a grin when she finished.

Nandara picked up the bone, looking it over.

"Clean repair. And quick. Well done, Neesha."

Neesha smiled, always glad to accept praise. But she knew this was only the start. Putting together matter, like bone from a corpse, was nothing. Mending living tissue in a living specimen... Well, that was something else entirely. Setting a bone on a living patient was not as simple as pushing two pieces back together. And healing speed had to be considered, as well as the patient's comfort level. It took far more energy to do.

But for the sake of her exams, putting lunch back together would suffice.

"Can we move on to larger flesh wounds?" Neesha asked.

Nandara looked thoughtfully at the bone in her hand. "I'd like to see a bit more work with minor wounds first."

"But I want to move on. There's a lot left to cover."

Nandara glanced at the stack of books Neesha had yet to conquer and then gave Neesha a pitying look. Neesha hated that look. These days, she saw it almost all the time from just about everyone she knew. Nandara sat next to her.

"I know you've convinced yourself you can be ready for your exam before the next moon. But Nee, you've got to be realistic. You're not ready. You're not going to be ready. Not before your child arrives."

Neesha glared, her body went cold. The fire in the hearth flared, and Nandara suppressed it without so much as a glance.

"These outbursts don't help your cause," Nandara said sternly. "Being a Guild wizard is about control, not just how powerful you are or what you can memorize. There's a remote chance you could pass the exam before you have your baby. But I will not let you risk your one chance at the Guild. I don't believe you really want to either."

"But how will I take care of myself? If I'm not in the Guild I can't expect work!"

"Your family isn't going to turn you out tomorrow. Your grandmother will probably let you stay as long as you like."

Nanny Shar hadn't spoken to Neesha since her foolish comment on her birthday three days ago, but there was no point in bringing that up.

"The sooner I can look after myself, the better for everyone."

"I understand, I really do. I never met your aunt, but I was there for the fallout of what she did. I know you want to be on your own, to avoid letting relationships sour to the point they did with Vyranna. But you know what will happen if you take the exam before you're ready."

Neesha closed her eyes and inhaled deeply, breathing back her anger and not letting her emotions alter the fire in the room. She had that control when she chose to use it. Something about her mother made her always want to go for the display of power.

"I'd never take the exam without your full confidence in my ability," Neesha said. "But can't we move forward a little faster?"

"Not if you want my confidence." Nandara's green eyes sparkled.

This got half a smile out of Neesha, but then she sighed and her expression fell.

"Am I really the fool everyone says I am for thinking I can do this on my own?"

Nandara pressed her lips together. "I think that depends on what sort of mother you are. And we'll need to wait until you've had some time at it to know.   You could probably manage, yes. But trying to do it all on your own is making things far more difficult than it needs to be. Do you see that?"

Neesha searched her mentor's expression for some hidden truth. She trusted Nandara, but hated when the woman echoed her mother's words. It meant either that Nandara wasn't being honest with her or her mother was right. Both options left a sour taste.

"I understand why everyone thinks it's going to be more difficult. But I think it will be worse to do things Mamma's way. Her way will be easier, but that doesn't make it better."

This drew a smile from Nandara. "Only you know your own heart, Nee. But you need to give more indication that you understand the consequences. Dionelle believes you act solely out of spite."

"Not solely." Neesha grinned.

"All right then, as long as you're certain. Let's get back to work."

Nandara broke the chicken bone again, this time using a mallet to crush part of it. Neesha settled back in to the race against impending motherhood.

CHAPTER FIVE

The waning summer weather was taking a turn toward autumn, a chill breeze prickling at Neesha's face as she left another lesson with Nandara. She only had a few left before the baby was expected. She wasn't going to make it into the Guild before then. She had come most of the way around to accepting it. She was sure it would bother her more if her thoughts weren't so consumed by her strong desire to have this pregnancy over with.

Even as the cool wind made her shudder, it numbed her many aches. She struggled down the laneway from Nandara's and out into the city, bowed forward no matter how hard she tried to walk upright. Like her womb was filled with a mountain instead of a tiny baby.

Her thoughts were foggy, like they had been at the start of it all. But this fog was caused by a different kind of exhaustion. She barely slept, never able to get comfortable. Everything ached. Every last inch of her felt bruised. The ground stabbed into her feet with each step. Her lower back felt aflame.

And so Neesha's concentration waned with each passing day. Instead of getting caught up in her studies, she fell further behind.

Neesha had done this to herself. Her mother was right, though Neesha didn't think she could ever confess her agreement. Neesha had been more than a willing partner to the men and women she had bedded, working to catch the attention of the one she expected was actually the babe's father.

She dug her hands into her lower back, thrusting her belly out farther as she tried desperately to stretch out the permanent ache. She rolled her shoulders back, trying to correct her ever-sagging posture and did her best not to waddle like a goose while she made her way out into the city and through the market square.

There was no dignity to be found.

Even if Nanny Shar wasn't talking to her, two weeks on, Neesha couldn't think of any place she'd rather be than home, curled up on something soft. And as she let the weariness distract her, she didn't pay attention to her route through the market. Tired as she was, she usually took a circuitous route through the square. It wasn't until Stone called to her that she realized she'd gone straight down the main avenue this time.

"Neesha, m'dear! Where have you been hiding?"

Wincing, Neesha turned. Even bent over the baskets he was arranging, Stone was exceptionally tall. He always had the finest berries and it was often hard to resist his table, even if talking with him grated on her nerves. But he smiled broadly under the bushy beard, his dark eyes alight as she approached.

"My apprenticeship is almost over," she said. "How have you been keeping?"

"Oh, busy as usual. Busier soon, with the harvest coming."

Neesha smiled and nodded politely, hoping she could get away quickly.

"I suppose you'll be busy with mothering soon." He watched her with a concerned and solemn expression. "Are you and the babe still healthy?"

"The midwife is pleased so far. No saying until the little one arrives."

Stone pursed his lips, scratching his scruffy cheek.

"I look forward to meeting the little one. You will let me know, won't you, if you need anything? Anything at all."

She smiled again, trying to keep her patience and cursing herself and her mother at the same time—herself for not paying attention to where she was going and putting herself in his path, and her mother for trying to match her with the man in the first place.

Neesha didn't hold anything against him, he was a sweet man—sweet and pathetic, like a lost puppy. He had never taken issue with Neesha's condition, and while she appreciated his concern and what tenuous friendship they had, she could not settle down with a man like him.

"Mamma and Pa are still doing good by me," Neesha said. They hadn't thrown her out entirely, so it wasn't a complete lie.

"I'm pleased to hear that."

He sounded a little more surprised by her news than she would have liked. She wondered if Bly wasn't talking to more than just their mother, or if her mother had reached new levels of desperation and was still scheming with Stone to have him marry her.

"Why don't you take some berries." He held a basket out to her.

"Thank you, Stone, but I really couldn't. Mamma has some berries in her garden. Not as good as yours, of course, but whose are?"

Stone smiled, broad and truly pleased, and Neesha couldn't help notice how much more alive he seemed when he saw her, when she showed him even the smallest kindness. It only made her feel worse for rejecting him. Made her wish she had the energy for rudeness. Made her wish he'd understand and move on.

She managed to extricate herself from the conversation and quickly made her way north, finally exiting the city and relieved to feel the dirt under her boots. She hadn't ever minded before, but the more cumbersome her load became, the harder it got to walk on the city's cobblestone streets. But even so, she wouldn't consider missing her lessons, and not only because it helped her escape the tensions at home. Difficult as the walk was becoming, it was blessedly quiet. Strenuous, yes, but there was peace to it too. As much as she loved her time with Nandara and all that she learned, she craved silence in a way she never had before.

When she was utterly alone, there was no one to judge her.

Out in the fields, silence wrapped around Neesha like a warm blanket, with no sounds around her but the wind through the crops and her feet on the dirt track. Even her mind's internal chatter had gone quiet. These were the moments she waited for every day. She'd just really sunk down into it when a dark shape passed overhead and engulfed her in shadow. She glanced up to see the black dragoness her mother loved so much and clenched her jaw, knowing the beast was heading to her house. Two smaller males silently glided overhead in the dragoness's wake, one of them was grey and the other so blue he nearly disappeared against the sky. She recognized them both by their colouring and knew that the cerulean one was the dragoness's mate. She'd heard him play dragonsong once and it had nearly moved her to tears, though she would never admit that to her mother.

She crossed her arms, resting them on the shelf of her belly, and stomped onward, contemplating stopping in someone's field until she saw the dragons leave.

A wagon clattered up behind her, surprising her out of her dark thoughts, and she stepped to the side of the dirt track to let it pass, wondering what the hurry was. But as the wagon approached, it slowed. She tensed when Ondias, her mother's best friend, hailed her. She turned as Ondias's wagon stopped beside her. The woman was frumpy at best, even if she did have the loveliest red hair Neesha had ever seen, but the seemingly permanent scowl didn't help the woman's overall countenance. Her hazel eyes were sharp, taking Neesha in with a quick glance.

"Come on. I'll give you a ride home."

Neesha wanted to say no, but the urgency in Ondias's voice made her curious about what was going on. She'd only once seen the results of the woman's frightening temper and decided that it was not the time to be contrary.

"Thank you." Neesha climbed in, grateful when Ondias leaned down to help her.

Ondias whipped the horse back into a trot so quickly that Neesha nearly toppled back over her seat and into the back of the wagon.

"By the moons, O, what's going on? You trying to knock the damned baby out of me right here?"

Ondias gave her a hard, oblique look, shrugging her long red braid off her shoulder as she did, and returned her focus back to the road. Neesha had no idea what she'd said to upset the woman, or why she was urgently chasing the dragons down. Neesha pulled her cloak around her shoulders and watched the farm approach in the distance.

The dragons were out in the front field with Dionelle when Neesha and Ondias arrived. Ondias pulled her wagon around the back and ducked into the stone house to retrieve Dionelle's firecloak before making her way to the meeting out in the yard. The large dragoness, a slice of deepest night in their back lane, crouched to be nearly eye level with the two women. The male dragons sat on their haunches, alert.

Neesha wanted nothing more than to go into the old farmhouse and sleep for the rest of the day. The dragons and Ondias crowding the yard to speak with Dionelle was common as breathing, but something about this felt different. There was urgency to it that Neesha hadn't seen before. With a sigh, she went into the farmhouse to get the purple cloak that had caused so much trouble on her birthday. She came tentatively out to the front yard, knowing well enough to stay off to the side until she'd been invited to join them.

Neesha heard only a few snatches of the conversation, something about the north, before the conversation fell silent on her approach. The black dragoness nodded her into the conversation, and Neesha bowed as she moved next to her mother.

"Greetings, Mistress."

Neesha had only bothered to learn the barest minimum of polite dragon interactions, but she knew enough to always use caution. She carefully held out the robe slung over her arm and took a moment to choose her words to keep from enraging the beast.

"I know my mother would never buy unsanctioned skins, but I thought it proper to check with you that the robe not offend you—not a dear comrade or anything—before I actually wear it."

The dragoness nodded in appreciation.

"This was a dragon known to me, but only just. A juvenile lost in a battle to the far east."

Neesha couldn't stop her jaw from hanging open. Who would be foolish enough to war with dragons? She assumed the responsible party had been reduced to ash.

"You may wear your gift without offense. We know which dragons are taken under sanction and which are not."

"Thank you, Mistress." Neesha shrugged into the robe and watched on as they continued the conversation.

"She won't listen and I don't know how to make her see," Dionelle said.

A ball of ice dropped into Neesha's gut as she initially assumed Dionelle was talking about her. But that would be no concern of the dragons. This must be about Lady Zyx. Neesha tried not to notice the way Ondias gave her another hard look at her mother's comment.

Neesha was grateful that her mother's best friend spent most of her time away from Pasdale, usually at the dragon city or off in other distant lands to spread her dragon knowledge. In the time since Ondias and Dionelle had first become friends, Ondias had become *the* academic authority on dragons. She was often gone as a result, had been gone since the spring, in fact.

"Shall we speak with the lady directly?" the dragoness asked.

"I don't know that it would do any good. She already knows that my messages come from you," Dionelle said. "Those raids, spreading in the northeast now, have not helped the cause. It casts suspicion on the words I deliver to her from you."

The dragoness scowled and bared some of her massive, glinting teeth. A mouthful of swords. "If it is even true that dragons are attacking humans, it is none of my kin. The Superiors maintain strict adherence to our accords with humans."

"Mistress, I know. But we need some kind of proof. Identifying those dragons would—"

"The accounts change every time we try to investigate. This is a minor concern. We have much bigger threats from the north."

Dionelle took a deep breath, sagging a little. "I can't make her see. Not with the evidence I've given her so far. We need more."

The urgency of their conversation was surprising. Dionelle had been frustrated of late because she wasn't being as valued as she was used to—Neesha to blame—but she'd never displayed this kind of despair. Ondias was usually relaxed, and to see her so tense was unsettling.

"By the time Draxli's movements reach her from human mouths, his host will be nearly upon her. She has no scouts in the northern territories beyond the kingdom."

"That's what dragons are for." Dionelle rubbed her temples. "The king has been insistent that Draxli isn't ambitious enough on his own to be capable of something like this. Lady Zyx is being far too complacent."

The dragoness growled impatiently, a low grumble like distant thunder resonating from deep in her chest.

"Could you convince her to send some scouts north?" Neesha asked and immediately fell apologetically silent when the others suddenly looked her way. She always forgot not to speak out of turn when the dragons were around. Her feet had gone numb from the walking and standing, her ankles were on fire, but curiosity kept her rooted in place. She pressed her hand into her back and shifted her weight.

"We could try," Dionelle said. "But Draxli is moving swiftly, more swiftly than he should be able to. By the time she got scouts to his location and any messages back from them, the host would be too close for her to act."

"Who is Draxli?"

"Draxli Dunham," Ondias said through gritted teeth.

Neesha felt suddenly numb.

"But... he was exiled." She looked apologetically to the dragoness, who allowed her interruption so far. "What in the name of the moons is he doing with a whole host? He's raised an army?"

Draxli Dunham had been a tyrant, his lady wife even worse by all accounts, once vexing this very dragoness into flaming Dionelle and then making Dionelle stand naked through the rest of the meeting. That, apparently, had been one of their kinder moments. Lord Draxli had been exiled by the king before Neesha had been born. Lady Karth had been executed for treason. All of it something to do with how Dionelle had been pulled into the fire realm, but Neesha had never cared enough to listen to the story before.

Ondias and Dionelle shared a quick glance, but it was the dragoness who answered.

"He has an army with frightening capabilities, levelling whole cities in hours, and he is moving swiftly toward Pasdale. He seems intent on revenge, and has been quite persuasive in stirring up anti-dragon sentiment."

"He's already near the kingdom's northern borders," Ondias said hastily. "I was just with them on their latest reconnaissance." She nodded to the dragons. "I've seen the host firsthand, and it was astounding. Their numbers alone can be managed, but they have been neutralizing dragon power in ways we don't understand yet."

Neutralize dragons? Neesha blinked rapidly, her thoughts trying to catch up to Ondias's words. She wouldn't have considered such a thing possible. She glanced at the massive dragoness, far larger than any house with talons longer than Neesha was tall.

How could someone *neutralize* dragons?

Whatever power could do that was headed their way. The chill autumn breeze suddenly held no comfort. Neesha shivered.

"But if you've seen this army firsthand, won't Lady Zyx listen to you?" Neesha asked.

"I just returned," Ondias said. "That's what we were discussing."

"I think it's worth seeking audience with the lady," Dionelle said.

"I'm not *your* daughter," Neesha said to Ondias. "Surely your friendship with us doesn't mar you in the same way."

Dionelle and Ondias shared the same surprised glance as before, and Neesha glowered, waiting to see what they'd come up with next. She wanted to indulge her anger, but fear bullied it aside. She was still hung up on dragons being neutralized. It was suddenly very clear why her mother had been so frantic over Neesha's situation. Neesha's pulse raced at the thought. If Draxli's force could neutralize dragons, what hope did the rest of them have?

"Lady Zyx may very well entertain the possibilities now that she's got a new source," Ondias said.

"If they mean to bring a war to us, why won't Lady Zyx take the threat seriously?"

"She's thought my warnings were a desperate grasp at regaining influence," Dionelle said. "Do you see now?"

Neesha's body hummed with rage at her mother's accusation, but she also did see, now, exactly what her mother had meant all along.

"Should I come with you?" Neesha asked, biting back her anger. "What if I spoke to the lady?"

"What could you hope to accomplish with that?" Dionelle asked.

What indeed? Neesha clenched her jaw and stared at the ground for a moment. Something was neutralizing dragons and Lady Zyx and the king were listening to none of it because it came from Dionelle, a woman whose daughter was a disgrace.

Neesha rested a trembling hand over the swell of her stomach.

"I could convince her that what I've done shouldn't bear on you," she muttered.

The silence that followed was so deep that Neesha was certain she'd said something wrong. She half expected one of the dragoness's great hands to come smashing down on her. When she chanced to look up at the other two women, they stared at her in open shock.

"It's not your fault," Neesha said sullenly, scowling deeper. "Is Lady Zyx really so stupid? I thought she knew what Auntie was like. No one held Auntie's behaviour against Nanny."

The shocked silence spread, thickening like fog roiling in, and Neesha suddenly wanted to slap the surprise right off her mother's face. Cold seeping in around the edges of Neesha's thoughts pushed away her anger. Fear pushed the shame she had tried to suppress to the forefront of her mind. While Neesha wouldn't place all the blame on outdated notions of womanhood, she wouldn't believe the situation was entirely her fault. But still, there had to be something she could do.

She was grateful when her mother broke the silence.

"Your grandmother lived in a small village where everyone knew and saw the truth on a daily basis," Dionelle said gently. "Is that why you thought you could get away with the same?"

Neesha swallowed a hot lump. The sudden embarrassment only served to stoke her anger even more. She narrowed her eyes at her mother and clenched her jaw so tightly it hurt, but Neesha knew better than to disrespect her mother in front of the dragons.

"You could try talking to Lady Zyx," Dionelle said. "It certainly won't make things worse."

Neesha nodded and resumed staring at the ground, her cheeks hot.

"Will we be able to seek an audience with her before tomorrow?" Ondias asked.

"It's unlikely," Dionelle said.

Ondias nodded. "Just as well. I've barely been home a day and I'll never hear the end of it from Zev if I don't give him and the kids at least a little of my attention today. This is going to get worse before we manage it."

"We could end up doing a fair bit of travelling. You could stay home, couldn't you? I can manage if a trip to the dragon city is necessary."

Ondias pressed her lips into a line and looked out toward the western mountains. "I don't know."

"Though it's informal, Ondias is the dragon whisperer in our great city," the dragoness said. "Even sending you in her stead will be seen as a slight without good reason."

Ondias snorted. "My husband having his britches in a knot about all my travel isn't going to amount to a hill of beans for the Dragoness Superior."

Neesha barely suppressed an eye roll. How could Zev be out of sorts just because Ondias travelled so much? With her position and far-reaching influence, how could she be expected to be a homebody? And besides, their three children were the same age as Neesha's brothers, and their oldest, Lina, had recently finished her schooling. Husbands seemed like more trouble than they were worth.

It was especially irritating that Ondias herself had been in Neesha's place, pregnant and unwed. She and Zev had probably been headed toward marriage anyway, but the baby had sped it along. But marriage had been good enough for Ondias, so they all somehow thought it was good enough for Neesha.

And of course there was the tension between Neesha's own parents when her mother first became dragon whisperer for Pasdale.

No, husbands were nothing but a bother.

"In the meantime," Ondias continued, "I'll consult with Nandara and see if she has any ideas on their strength."

"It's elemental magic, isn't it?" Neesha glanced nervously to the dragoness. "To neutralize the dragons like that, they'd need to be working with another element. Wouldn't they?"

"Yes, that's likely," the dragoness said. "Air or water elementals could combat dragonflame. I have not spoken directly with the few dragons who have survived these attacks."

Neesha shivered. How many dragons had Draxli managed to *neutralize*? How had she missed how dire things were before?

"Child, you are a gifted pyromancer." The dragoness openly assessed her. "Your skill may be of value to us. We will speak with your mentor and gather more information before we plan our course of action. We may need to bring this to the Dragoness Superior and her counsel."

Neesha nearly interrupted with another question, but managed to bite her tongue. She pressed her lips together to keep back any further outbursts and wondered what the dragoness's last comment had meant. She didn't think the Dragoness Superior ever left the dragon city—did this mean they'd be venturing there? The prospect was fascinating and terrifying.

She hadn't considered the fact that she would have anything to offer in this battle. If she wasn't in the Guild, would she be allowed to do much? By her very nature, it was impossible not to use pyromancy, and she had been shown leniency on many of the Guild's usual rules for apprentices. After all, she had her mother watching over her when Nandara wasn't.

And if things were as bad as they seemed, would it matter if a pyromancer as powerful as Neesha was Guild-sanctioned or not?

Neesha sank into her thoughts and let the meeting with the dragons carry on as if she weren't there. She only half-listened, wondering at all the things she'd learned that might help stop Draxli's forces. There were things she shouldn't know how to do that she'd picked up while covertly watching Nandara. Could she use those?

She looked up only when Ondias headed back to her wagon, the immediate course of action having been decided. Dionelle would send a message to Lady Zyx seeking an audience, and Ondias would seek counsel from Nandara in the meantime. With nothing left to do but wait, Dionelle bid the dragoness and her blaze a farewell, and the three women braced themselves against the gale as the dragons took to the skies and disappeared over the northern horizon.

Neesha stood back, her robe draped over her arm, as her mother saw Ondias off. Once they were alone, Dionelle stood in front of Neesha, appraising her as if seeing her for the first time.

"That was quite the about-face from you."

"I'm not stupid, Mamma," Neesha snapped. "I know exactly what will happen to me if war comes to us—here in Pasdale—any time soon."

Dionelle closed her eyes and let out a long, slow breath.

"Neesha, darling, would it really cause you so much pain to be so reasonable a little more often?"

"I was never going to do things your way." Neesha crossed her arms.

"You can do things your own way," Dionelle said. "I've never expected you to be like me, or like your father, but it would have done us all some good if you'd at least been a little less like your aunt."

"Maybe she was right about some of it," Neesha snapped. "She was certainly right to be angry, but wrong in what she did with it. What if she was jealous not of you and Pa, but because you could be happy with what everyone around you expected of you while she couldn't?"

Dionelle blinked. "Is that what you feel? Is that why you're like this?"

"Like this?" Neesha tilted her head, trying to rein in the anger buzzing through her. "You mean angry at the unfair treatment? Yes, it's exactly why."

"I know it's hard for you, to look so much like me and have so many of the same abilities that I did, and yet be so very different. I know other people have certain expectations of you, and that isn't fair, but those are not the expectations I have. And surely this isn't the identity you really want to have, is it?"

She waved a hand in the general direction of Neesha's growing belly. Neesha folded her arms across herself, the robe shielding her from her mother's scrutiny. Dionelle's expression softened, that horrible pitying look lurking in her eyes.

"Nee, I want you to be yourself, and I don't think you have been. You've bent all your will toward spiting those who would paint you with the same brush as me or as your aunt, and have not left any energy for cultivating who you really are. I fear you may never find out."

"Mamma, I can't be myself. You won't let me. The *world* won't." Before she had time to think against it, she blurted, "I don't like men."

Dionelle gave her a wry look, briefly touching Neesha's belly. "I know that's not entirely true."

Neesha rolled her eyes. "*That* part is fine. It's their personalities I don't like. Having to spend the entire rest of my life with the same one would be a misery I can't even think to bear. If I really *must* get married, I'd truly rather have a wife."

Dionelle pressed her lips together, tapping her chin. Then she sighed and Neesha tensed, feeling cold.

"Nee, I wish you'd said something sooner. I could have helped you if I'd known even a couple of years ago."

Neesha grit her teeth. "Helped? How?"

"There are whole networks of people like you, making their own arrangements on marriage, or what looks like marriage. We could have found you suitors that way."

"And what, have some sort of sham marriage with some man as interested in me as I am in him?"

"That's one of the arrangements, yes." She shrugged helplessly.

"That's foolish!"

"I know." Dionelle sighed. "But it's what we've got to work with."

Dionelle paused and looked to the horizon where the dragons had disappeared before turning back to her daughter. She placed a hand on Neesha's shoulder and spoke gently.

"Things have changed irrevocably for you—you are soon going to be defined by that babe inside you. Becoming a mother is going to change everything—I can see that it's already begun. It will only get more difficult. I had the luxury of really growing into myself before you were born. I had support that you don't have."

"I don't need a husband." Neesha's words were full of frost and it was all she could do not to bare her teeth.

Dionelle sighed wearily. "You're going to find, very soon, that you do. Vyranna could get away with the independence she had because she wasn't a mother. The standard changes when you have a child. I'm not saying it's right, I'm just telling you what it's like."

Neesha's rage rose, a numbing heat that spread through her body and across her shoulders. She looked away as her shame rose with it.

"I tried to apologize to Nanny," she said, her voice small, constricted by oncoming tears.

"I know what you said seemed like a small thing to you, but she's never forgiven herself for what happened to Vyranna. Do you realize she thinks, even now, that she could have done something? That if she had only suffered through your aunt's abuse a little longer, things would have been different? Cusec remembers, and so do I, exactly how bad it was. Time has blurred the ugliness for Nanny Shar, and all she remembers is how she lost her daughter so soon after turning her out."

Neesha's lip trembled and she clenched her jaw against it, breathing deeply through the guilt until the threat of tears passed.

"Mamma, what can I do? If Nanny won't even talk to me, how can I apologize?"

"Words aren't going to fix all that you've done, Nee. You have to show her your remorse."

Neesha hung her head, breathing heavily and trying not to think much about her mother's words. The idea of having fallen out of favour with her grandmother was far too much to bear.

"Your grandmother has been silently suffering through all the foolish things you've done, partly because she's afraid turning her back on you will result in you following your aunt's path."

"I'm tired," Neesha said, all emotion drained out of her, leaving only the profound exhaustion she'd been burdened with for the last month or so, since the baby had begun growing rapidly.

This weariness ran deeper, and she was half-prepared to curl up in the grass. She longed for somewhere warm and soft to lie down and craved the solitude that Ondias and the dragons had robbed her of.

"Go rest," Dionelle said, her voice touched by exasperation once again, waving her hand dismissively.

Neesha wanted to make her mother understand but didn't have the strength. She pulled herself back into the farmhouse, leaving her robe lying across the back of one of the chairs by the hearth and curling up on the sofa in the main room. As soon as she lay down to rest, the baby began dancing a jig in her belly and Neesha draped her arm over it, wishing it would rest when she did.

At least she was somewhere soft and warm. Somewhere quiet. Somewhere her thoughts could collect themselves. She'd never admit to her mother that she was even half right, but if she proved her worth in the upcoming battle, maybe it would ease some of the tension. There had to be a middle ground, some compromise that would make her mother happy but keep Neesha out of the yoke of marriage.

She'd start with setting things right with Lady Zyx. Maybe that would be enough. And if not, she'd show them exactly what kind of pyromancer she was.

CHAPTER SIX

That desperately needed nap continued to elude Neesha, and it wasn't only the baby's acrobatics keeping her awake. A dozen aches and pains pinged through her body as she lay on the couch. Her emotions kept somersaulting over her thoughts. She couldn't stop replaying the conversation between her mother, Ondias and the dragoness. Anytime she thought about how they underestimated her, she'd end up with her fists clenched around her blanket and biting back a scream. But when she considered actually using her power in a battle, she felt lightheaded and giddy but cold with fear.

The fear was something new that she could easily cling to for motivation. Being a pyromancer made her a natural ally to the dragons. She knew little about dragon magic but pushed down thoughts of asking her mother for details. Still, there had to be so much she could learn from them. What would they be like in battle? Magnificent, probably.

She had accidentally learned a few things that she wondered if she could use to help the dragons. She didn't know much about war and using spellcraft in a battle, but she did know that she could combat other elements—that much Nandara had taught her. And then there was that new thing she'd been trying, something likely quite dangerous and also unique to her. Her nature as fireborn gave her an edge that no other elemental had.

Neesha hadn't realized she'd fallen asleep with her thoughts until she heard the clatter of dishes in the kitchen. She was groggy, still exhausted, and slowly lifted her head to see Nanny in the kitchen, preparing dinner.

"Nanny, let me help you." Neesha clumsily struggled to her feet and toddled into the kitchen.

Nanny silently continued chopping up vegetables and tossing them into the skillet. She had said nothing to Neesha since her doomed birthday party.

Neesha swallowed a hot lump in her throat. Nanny had been providing for her needs, bringing her things she clearly needed, doing the chores, and leaving food for her at mealtimes, although they didn't eat together. Nanny stealthily prepared and ate her meals without Neesha noticing, disappearing into her room or going over to the main house and leaving Neesha to eat alone.

This was much different than the solitude Neesha sought. This was loneliness that spoke volumes and indicated deep judgement that she resented.

"Nanny, please! I'm sorry. What I said was cruel and thoughtless. I didn't mean it."

"That doesn't make it any less hurtful! When are you going to learn that? You cut your mother far worse than this every single day."

Neesha's mouth fell open. This was far worse than the wounded silence that had enveloped them for days. But Nanny didn't afford Neesha the opportunity to respond. She stopped chopping in the middle of a carrot, thumped her knife down onto the cutting board, and walked briskly out the back door letting it swing shut, slamming behind her.

Neesha stood where she was for far longer than good sense allowed, hoping her grandmother would come back. She didn't. Neesha took the skillet off the heat and left it, not interested in eating. But knowing she needed to eat something, she took the chopped bits of carrot with her and went to sit on the front porch to nibble on the pieces.

When darkness fell with no sign of her grandmother, Neesha went to the main house, a large stone mammoth meant to contain the large family and made of stone to protect against the dangers of having pyromancers in the house. Neesha had started many accidental blazes in the farmhouse when she'd been younger, and she and Dionelle had caused the hearth to spew angry flames into the living room on several occasions when they'd argued, their emotions feeding on each other and working exponentially on the fire.

Neesha tapped at the door, hoping her appearance on the porch wouldn't cause too much friction. It was her mother who answered and that was a small blessing. She knew she wouldn't be able to face her father.

"Mamma, I want to show you something. You and Nanny. Will you come?"

Neesha saw refusal forming in her mother's expression, and she went cold, fearing her mother's prophecies of total isolation had finally come true, but at the last moment Dionelle's expression softened. She nodded and closed the door. Neesha wasn't entirely sure what to make of her mother's actions and stood on the porch for a moment to see if Dionelle and Nanny would join her. She realized they weren't coming right away, and she went back to the farmhouse, a dark, lurking shadow, something empty and ominous where it had always been so welcoming.

She pushed in the back door, felt her way across the black room, and lit the lamp in the kitchen. She pulled some of the fire from the wick, letting it burn in the palm of her hand, a soothing, warm sensation when everything else in the world always seemed so cold. She carried the fire with her to the candles and lamps around the main floor. She held her burning palm near the wicks and gently blew a few sparks to light them. When she reached the hearth, filled with cold ashes and dark embers, she placed a fresh log inside. Gathering her will, she cast the last of the flame from her hand into the hearth where the dry old wood immediately erupted with light. She rolled up her sleeves and worked carefully to build a large fire, less for the heat than for what she intended. A larger fire would make it easier to show her family what she could do.

Her body ached but she remained kneeling in front of the fire, watching it closely, feeling the warmth it provided and growing nervous as the minutes stretched on with no sign of her mother or grandmother. Finally, the back door creaked open, and she stood, stretching the dull ache from her back. She walked around the stairs jutting into the middle of the house to see Nanny and Dionelle cautiously entering the kitchen.

Neesha didn't say anything and beckoned them to join her. Both women stood expectantly in the middle of the room, waiting to see what she had to say, waiting to be disappointed. She'd show them!

Neesha gathered her will and faced her family.

"I'm sorry, Mamma, that I didn't pay attention to your warnings sooner—about the north. I didn't realize who was behind it all. But I think I can help. I want to show you what I can do—the kinds of weapons I can wield, though clumsily at the moment."

Dionelle frowned and crossed her arms.

"Nee, you shouldn't be using any weapons, not yet. You need to be a Guild member to work that kind of magic."

"Nandara taught me the theory. I've read plenty about it and have been practicing on my own, so I'd be ready to begin it as soon as I gained entry to the Guild. But Guild or not, I'm going to defend myself—to defend *us*—if war comes to us. If you'll let me, I want to help the dragons stop it from ever reaching here."

Her mother's frown deepened, but out of concern.

"Here, I'll show you." Neesha pulled on her dragon skin robe and knelt in front of the fire, focusing on its intensity and casting the same spell she'd seen Nandara do so many times. The fire and the spell washed over her, filling her with warm peace.

"No," her mother whispered fearfully, but Neesha was too intent on her own actions to heed Dionelle. How could there be any harm in something that relaxed her so deeply?

The fire erupted with light, so bright Neesha could barely look at it, but she narrowed her eyes to slits, squinting hard against it, remaining focused and continuing her hissed siren song. She had a demon here, but most elementals could call them—she could do something far more impressive than that. She tingled with anticipation.

Spreading her arms in welcome, she altered the call of her spell, drawing the demon forward as she drew the fire toward her. There was a moment of intense light, blotting out the whole of the world, searing heat numbing her senses, and then everything spun back into the same dimness she was used to from the farmhouse. As the world around her dulled, the demon's heat electrified her, her whole body tingling like a gentle, constant lightning bolt.

It was harder to maintain the focus on her surroundings and on the demon, but she had done this before and it was easier every time. She stood to face her mother and grandmother, not quite able to parse their expressions, but unable to contain the grin at showing them what she could do. Anyone who worked with an elemental demon could be possessed, but Neesha was in complete control, even if only barely. That giddy heat kept trying to pull her under, but she rode the wave of it. Her hand was already outstretched, palm up, fingers curled almost like claws, and she pulled fire from the very air, a burning ball of heat in her palm like when she'd lit the candles, only this flame hadn't been created from other flame.

It had come from nothing.

"See?" Neesha said. "Surely I can use this against Draxli."

"Oh my stars," Nanny gasped, wobbling sideways and sinking into the large armchair.

It took a moment for Neesha to realize that her grandmother was sobbing. What could be wrong? She staggered forward, always having to concentrate on her body with the distraction the demon provided. She wanted to show the two women that it was all right, but they instantly recoiled, Nanny climbing over the arm of the chair to retreat.

"Neesha, stop!" Dionelle shouted, eyes wide, body tense.

Neesha paused in the middle of the room, watching them closely and not liking the looks of horror. This was supposed to impress them. How had she disappointed them so badly again? Maybe they didn't understand what she had done, what she was doing. It would be easier to explain without the presence of the demon constantly wearing on her, trying to take control, so she turned back to the hearth and released the creature back to its realm.

She staggered, collapsing to one knee, feeling cold and empty, the exhaustion hitting her harder than usual. Containing the demons was a demanding task, but with the baby sapping her energy, it was more daunting than ever.

She pushed herself to her feet, her knees creaking and back aching, and faced them, hoping they would be reassured.

"Don't you see?" she asked, baffled by the horror in their expressions.

Dionelle held her sobbing mother while eyeing Neesha with utter disdain. "Neesha, do you have any idea what you just did?"

"I took in a fire demon." She tried to keep her tone neutral, though all she wanted to do was boast. "I held it—it didn't hold me."

They needed to understand the difference. Any elemental could call a demon and use its strength, anyone at all could be possessed by one, but only she had the power to remain in full control, wielding the power of a demon for her own use and of her own will.

"Heavens, child, of course we could see that you were possessed. Have you forgotten whose presence you're in?"

Dawning realization suddenly burst through Neesha's mind as she remembered how difficult it had been for her grandmother when her grandfather had been possessed. They hadn't known until Dionelle had been pulled wholly into the fire realm what had actually happened to Draidel, but of course her grandmother would recognize a demon possession for what it really was, having lived with it for so long.

"I'm sorry, Nanny. I should have warned you what I was doing."

"You shouldn't be trying anything so incredibly foolish and dangerous," Dionelle snapped.

"I—Mamma, I don't know why you're so angry."

"It's not only what you put your grandmother through with that stunt. Have you forgotten entirely how I ended up in the fire realm in the first place?"

Neesha's cheeks flushed with unusual heat, and she looked down at the floor, unable to hold her mother's intense gaze. Dionelle had said she remembered little of the demon attack that had killed her mentor, but she had spoken of the way the fire had flared intensely before claiming her. Neesha suddenly felt foolish for not considering how distressing this power might be. Had she always been so lacking in empathy for her family?

"Mamma, I'm sorry. I forgot. I was just so excited to show you... I can help!"

"Neesha, please, promise me you'll never do that again," Dionelle said, her voice thick with anger and fear.

Neesha's mouth fell open and she shook her head. "But I'm just getting good at it! And it can help."

"Oh my stars, how many times have you done that?"

Neesha paused, considering. "That was the fifth time. It was an accident the first time. I'd seen Nandara call them so many times through the work she does that I wanted to try it one night. It was maybe two months ago. Mamma, why are you upset with me? This is something I can use to help stop Draxli."

"Five times," Dionelle said in terrible awe, shaking her head. Her intense gaze, all fire and shining blue, never once left Neesha. She didn't seem to hear anything else that Neesha had said. "Don't you realize the dangers you're bringing on yourself?"

"I'm in control, Mamma. It can't hurt me. I can use its power."

Dionelle closed her eyes and pressed her tented fingers against her lips while Nanny sank back into the chair, still weeping.

"Neesha, there are so many reasons why what you just did was incredibly dangerous, particularly if you believe you were really in full control of that demon. You were no more in control of that demon than I am ever in control of the dragons."

"The dragons would never hurt you."

Dionelle's eyebrows shot up in surprise before she scowled angrily.

"The dragoness has set me ablaze before, and you know that. Even now, an arrogant misstep could spell my end. If I anger her, if I offend her deeply enough, she will end me. Make no mistake about that. It may look like she and I are dear friends, and in some ways we are, but Neesha... she is still a dragon! She is still dangerous and has a mind that I will never fully understand."

Neesha fell quiet, sobered by her mother's frank lecture. Somehow, she had always believed the dragoness was more like some domesticated farm animal, albeit much larger. Dangerous like a bull, but predictable when precautions were taken.

"The demons are even less understood and even less predictable," Dionelle said. "It wants nothing more than to take full control over you. Are you going to try to tell me you didn't feel it trying?"

Neesha shook her head. "It tried, but I didn't let it."

"Your demon essence allows you a small measure of protection against that, but make no mistake, that the protection is indeed small. And who can say how much it enrages them to take possession of a body and then be held prisoner rather than have a new toy to play with. That is all we are to the demons, mere trifles."

"And the baby!" Nanny lamented.

"Yes, what of your child?" Dionelle stood and moved to the centre of the room, but dared not get any closer, like Neesha was some wild animal. "I am the way I am because my father was possessed. Some of that initial essence remains in you, but your powers far exceed mine because you were still developing in my womb while we both lived on the powers of the fire realm. Your essence is strong, no one denies that, and much of it is going to be passed to your child. What further damage is being done—how much stronger is your child's demon essence going to be because of this?"

Neesha grew numb and sat heavily on the edge of the hearth, trembling slightly at her utter lack of foresight.

"Stop these possessions," Dionelle said. "It is far too dangerous for you and your babe alike. May the stars show you mercy and your child not be born entirely demon. You are going to birth pure flame if you are not careful."

Silent tears spilled down Neesha's cheeks, and she tried to blink them away as she addressed her mother.

"But I can help with Draxli."

"Not by using demons. And certainly not until we've brought Ondias's new information to Lady Zyx. We can only hope that she will see reason. In the meantime, I want you to talk to Nandara about this and see how she thinks it may affect your child. You really need to purge the essence, Neesha. I know it's powerful, but you will still be strong without it. I am proof of that."

"No!" Neesha jumped to her feet, heart pounding. "I am not renouncing this power for anything. This power is what I am—all I have."

Her tears came more swiftly, rage and shame mingling into a perfect storm. Unable to face her family in the grip of her emotions, she turned and fled to her room, angry that Dionelle never understood what the power meant to her—how it was the only piece of her identity that was really hers anymore. And still her mother put Neesha's needs last. That everyone kept putting the babe's needs above her own made Neesha all the more furious.

Of course, she was also ashamed that she hadn't realized the dangers of the demon possession sooner. She would not call upon them needlessly, but it was an option, a powerful weapon to use if the need arose. Why couldn't her mother see the value in using that kind of power against Draxli's forces? She was trying to do things her mother's way, or at least a step in that direction. She was trying to help, trying to be responsible. And still it wasn't good enough.

Now more than ever, she needed to be on her own and out of this house.

But they were going to see Lady Zyx tomorrow. Maybe Neesha could at least convince her to see value in Neesha's skill.

CHAPTER SEVEN

Neesha's soft footfalls echoed off the marble of the cavernous palace hallways. Soft whispers from clusters of gathered courtiers did the same. She had fallen silent within moments of arriving and walked quietly next to her mother and Ondias. Neither of them noticed, their conversation not pausing for an instant as they came in. Neesha couldn't focus on their words, though it seemed to centre on the conversation they were about to have with Lady Zyx.

Neesha wasn't sure how she'd never been to the palace before, at least not that she remembered. Even if there wasn't any reason for her to come with her mother on business, she'd never been with Nandara, either. While most of Neesha's apprenticeship involved studying dusty books in Nandara's cramped home library, there were occasional field trips. But none of them had ever been on official court business.

So many of the adults in her life were on the palace grounds regularly, including Ondias who frequently consulted with the lady, and her husband Zev, who had served the court since before the Dunhams' fall. She knew that their daughter Lina, who was a couple of years younger than Neesha, was at the palace now and then. Of course, Lina wasn't an embarrassment to her family. Perhaps if Neesha had been friends with the girl the way their parents had undoubtedly expected, she wouldn't be such an embarrassment either.

Neesha pressed her lips together, deepening her silence.

The other two women stopped outside a pair of large, honey-coloured doors. Dionelle had a word with one of the guards out front. The man slipped through the doors, gone only a moment, but the trio remained where they were. Waiting. They were set to meet with the lady in moments.

Neesha had tamed her wild fringe of hair in a long, thick braid and wore the cleanest, newest garments that would fit her, including the new boots and cloak she'd received for her birthday. She'd even chosen to wear the pendant Breen had given her. She wasn't sure why she was so nervous, but supposed she had convinced herself that she could somehow sway the lady in one conversation and undo all the damage she had done, instantly inspiring the lady to believe what her mother and Ondias had to report. A swift end to the threat, war averted, and the day saved.

Neesha sighed wearily at her own naïveté and hoped she wouldn't make things any worse.

They were finally called in and Neesha was relieved that there weren't many others in the room. Like the halls they'd been through, this room was large and airy, bright with torchlight from wall sconces and bright sunshine filtering through skylights. Yet every rustle of fabric echoed. Neesha softened her steps even more.

She wasn't sure what she expected, but this wasn't it. There were a pair of guards at the door, and one at the foot of the dais where the throne was. A serving girl of some kind stood next to Lady Zyx's throne.

Neesha, as she'd been briefed to do, bowed before the dais, in perfect unison with Ondias and Dionelle. She held her breath and concentrated on holding still, staring at the tile mosaic under her feet. Lady Zyx didn't leave them there for long, calling them forward after a beat. Keeping her head bowed and peeking up, Neesha got a good look at the lady. She sat erect in her throne, but gently so, with easy poise, her lavender robes draped to her feet and her grey eyes watchful but kind. Her silver-blonde hair was plaited around her head, much like the crown she wore.

Lady Zyx watched her closely and Neesha worried about what would come next, what had to come next.

"Is this your daughter?" Lady Zyx asked, glancing to Dionelle.

"Of course I'm her daughter, m'lady," Neesha blurted out, having decided the night before, when she'd first found out she'd play audience to the lady, that this was the course she would take. "Your dragon whisperer doesn't suffer the presence of unwed harlots unless she absolutely has to. And really, how many of your subjects are this white?"

"Neesha!" Dionelle gasped.

The other three women stared at Neesha, and she made out the horror on her mother's face in the periphery. She watched Lady Zyx too closely to really give notice. Lady Zyx's mouth was pressed into a firm line. The silence that followed was deep as a winter night, broken by Ondias.

"How does this help?" she asked in an angry whisper.

"The lady may as well see me for what I really am. And see how powerless my mother has been in the face of it."

Neesha watched the lady, even though Dionelle had grabbed her arm and was trying to force her to look at her.

"What is the meaning of this?" Lady Zyx asked tersely, turning her attention to Dionelle. "I was anticipating news from the dragons."

"M'lady, please, you have my sincerest apologies. The girl said she wanted to help. She even displayed a little bit of sense and a healthy dose of fear. I just—" Dionelle shook her head helplessly and glared at Neesha.

"You just do the best you can, and I blast right through your will like a firestorm," Neesha said defiantly. She was still watching the lady, waiting to see if the woman would address her directly or not. "M'lady, this is who I am. This is what I am. You know that I am a powerful pyromancer, and I am my own force of nature. My mother has been able to tame me just as well as she could tame a prairie storm. Any scorn she receives on my account is so foolishly undeserved. I would think my brothers' perfect conduct would be evidence enough that she's not a failure as a mother, wife, and model courtier. If anything, I'm a failure as a daughter."

Lady Zyx faced Neesha, who hoped the woman would speak. She only ground her teeth and glared.

Dionelle had a solid grip on Neesha and wrested her farther away from the lady, getting in between the two of them so that Neesha had no choice but to look at her mother. Neesha could look over her mother, just barely, if she wanted to, but decided the point had been made. Dionelle was trying to force Neesha out of the room, but even without the weight of pregnancy, Neesha outweighed her thin mother significantly. She was broad like her father and always seemed far bigger when she was next to Dionelle.

But Ondias had a little more heft to her and she drove one of her hands against Neesha's shoulder and pushed her back. Neesha had no choice but to back away or be knocked over. She tried to dig her heels in, tried to get a good view of Lady Zyx to see if the outburst had been successful, but the combined efforts from Ondias and Dionelle were too much. Neesha continued walking backward, forced away by Ondias, while Dionelle turned and bowed apologetically.

"M'lady, my sincerest apologies. I truly believed she'd found some sense, or I never would have requested you suffer through her presence. It's not a mistake I will make again."

"I do believe the girl has made her point." Lady Zyx looked away from Neesha and addressed Dionelle. "If she's done with the outbursts, she may as well stay."

"She'll interrupt plenty if she remains," Dionelle said.

"It's true," Neesha called.

This earned a wry smirk from Lady Zyx. "Sometimes empathy is earned only through hard lessons. I can see why she draws comparisons to your sister."

Dionelle sighed wearily and glanced back to where Ondias kept Neesha partially restrained.

"It has been this way since she was a little girl, first in school, and her heritage as fireborn and daughter of a dragon whisperer began to press on her."

"She has certainly shown me that it is not my place to judge the difficulties that beset a mother."

Neesha instinctively opened her mouth to argue but let it hang open for a moment as she processed what the lady had said. She pressed her lips together, and the tension uncoiled from her body. She hadn't even considered it a factor that Lady Zyx had never conceived children of her own. It was a simple thing, but it explained so much. Neesha had always assumed that people would understand how difficult a time Dionelle had with her children, like most parents did at some point or another. At least the lady was considering the fact that Neesha was, in fact, her own person and not merely some extension of her mother.

Ondias shook her head and walked back to the dais to join Dionelle. Neesha remained where she was while the lady addressed her mother.

"You have reports, then?" Lady Zyx asked. "You didn't only come here so that your daughter could insult me."

"No, m'lady, but if you wish for Neesha to see time in the dungeons for her insolence, I will not resist my Lady's wishes."

A cold twinge slid down Neesha's spine. She raised an eyebrow at this, wondering if they were having some fun at her expense or if she'd really said something that would earn her time in the dungeons. Would they jail a pregnant woman over something so trivial?

"If she can maintain a sense of decorum, I will overlook her earlier missteps."

Dionelle bowed. "Thank you. My Lady is too kind."

"Now, then, what word from the dragons?"

Dionelle began explaining, but quickly yielded to Ondias, who had actually been with the dragons in the north. Neesha had already heard all of this, but grew cold hearing it again, especially when Ondias recounted the size of the army.

"There are perhaps five thousand—not an outrageously large host, but still a deep concern," Ondias said. "The real problem is how quickly they move and how destructive they are. The dragoness has reported a loss of five of her kind in the fighting."

Lady Zyx sat up straighter, watching Ondias as if she expected the woman to reverse her statement and admit to a lie.

"We suspect elemental magic," Dionelle said.

"That is alarming," Lady Zyx said. "I know my cousin the king is reluctant to believe that Draxli could gain so much support, reluctant to believe that he has the ambition to accomplish such a feat. But the king didn't have to live with the fallout of Draxli's rule. He was not here when the Dunhams were seized and did not see the absolute grief that overtook Draxli when Karth was sentenced to death." Lady Zyx tapped her hand against one knee. "Draxli loved her. Say what you will about them, he loved that woman in all her sadistic glory. He was only ambitious for her, but he was always a scheming man."

Lady Zyx tented her fingers and rested her chin against them, staring thoughtfully across her throne room. She fixed her gaze on Dionelle.

"I assume Nandara has been briefed."

"Yes, m'lady. She is working to determine which element Draxli is using—the dragoness has suggested air or water most likely."

Lady Zyx nodded, still thoughtful. "We don't have time to scout," she said. "We will have to prepare defenses on the northern border without truly knowing what we face. Dionelle, can you negotiate for dragon reinforcements? I assume that by the time Draxli's forces reach the kingdom, we'll have a better idea of what we face."

"Yes, m'lady, I believe the dragons are eager to help, especially after losing so many of their own."

"He hates them, you know," Lady Zyx said. "He blames the dragons even more than you for what happened to he and Karth."

Neesha grew numb, having expected that Draxli only wanted his seat of power back, not that he was targeting specific individuals in acts of revenge. If he was looking to avenge himself and his dead wife, Dionelle and her family would also be targets.

"I want to help," Neesha called, as her mother went through the formalities of saying goodbye.

"Oh heavens, child, you really are insufferable!" Lady Zyx snapped.

"Insufferable *and* powerful."

"Yes, you're a pyromancer, I am aware. Your involvement is not up to me, but your mentor and your mother."

"They're not going to let me," Neesha said. "You're the leader here, you can override them."

Lady Zyx gave her a sharp look, and Neesha clenched her jaw against any further outbursts.

"I preside over Pasdale," Lady Zyx said, her tone slow and careful. "Your involvement in these matters must be sanctioned by the Wizards Guild, which is beyond my dominion. You must take up the narrative with your mentor."

Neesha didn't miss the gentle warning in the woman's tone or the finality of the discussion. She knew better than to argue, especially after the threat of the gaol. She bowed and remained silent, standing patiently behind her mother and Ondias as they concluded their meeting and whisked her out of the room.

But Lady Zyx hadn't outright denied Neesha's request, merely deferred authority. So as Ondias and Dionelle, each on either side of her, gripped her arms and led her out of the palace, glaring icily, Neesha considered the best way to convince Nandara to let her help in battle.

CHAPTER EIGHT

It had been many years since Neesha had heard the dragons cry out on their approach, and she stood on the farmhouse porch, watching them draw nearer while her mother pulled on a cloak and went out into the downpour to meet them. Neesha wanted to join them, to hear what was going on, especially after she had been allowed to participate in the last meeting, but her mother struggled through the muck, nearly losing a boot to it, and Neesha knew that if she fell in her condition, she would be stuck there until the rains stopped. If they stopped. After two days of steady downpour, it was difficult to say when that would happen.

"These are troubled times," Nanny said from behind her, coming to stand on the porch and watch Dionelle receive the black dragoness, an emerald and gold dragon, and an orange dragon who looked like flame come alive.

"Is it the war coming?" Neesha asked.

"I haven't seen rains like these since your mother was in the fire realm."

That was troubling, indeed, and Neesha looked back out to where her mother stood. Dionelle's time in the fire realm had thrown the elements out of balance and nearly ended the world. Is that what this unending rain meant—the end of the world?

The dragoness nimbly plucked Dionelle from the muck and, with little more than a lean, was across the yard and depositing the mud-caked woman at the foot of the stairs.

"Thank you, Mistress, you are a true comrade." Dionelle bowed. The dragoness snorted, seemingly amused by Dionelle's overly formal manner, and took to the skies, the gale of her wings nearly knocking Dionelle into the stairs. Neesha and Nanny both gripped the porch railings to steady themselves. The dragons' cries rattled Neesha's teeth as they disappeared into the gloom.

"What's going on?" Nanny asked.

Dionelle chewed on her bottom lip as she made her way up the steps, thoroughly soaked and covered in mud nearly up to her hips.

"The rain is unnatural, as we've feared. The dragoness and her blaze have been circling it all day, and she says that it is self-perpetuating and stationary in the valley. The weather beyond is autumnal, but not nearly so wet."

"There's more," Neesha said.

"There was just an attempt on Lady Zyx," Dionelle said gravely. "She was injured in the attack, but she is able to lead. Not that she can lead anyone anywhere. Her troops have not been able to leave for the northern passes to defend the border because the way has been flooded. They can barely leave the city for all the mud." Dionelle gestured to the mess on her legs and feet.

Neesha couldn't imagine trying to get a wagon or even a mule through such conditions. Walking would be very difficult. They had received word at all solely because of the dragons, who were capable of flying far beyond the reach of the weather.

"This is an attack," Neesha said.

Dionelle nodded, still worrying at her lip.

"So it's water demons," Neesha said. "Or else they'd be sending a gale to topple us. Water like this can be far too much for a dragon to handle—it can drown their fires. But enough fire can evaporate the water."

"You are not to be involved in this," Dionelle said quickly. "You are not qualified, and the Guild would discipline you—possibly bar you future entry—if you were to perform spells beyond your station."

"Blast my station and their stuffy old rules! What good will the Guild's approval do me if we're all drowned and dead?" Neesha snapped, crossing her arms and glaring out into the rain. "I can help, so let me. I won't stand back and do nothing."

Dionelle ground her teeth, looking out through the curtain of water toward the city proper.

"Some of the Guild wizards made it into the city before the rains made travel impossible," Dionelle said. "Nandara is with them, and they will determine their next course of action. Nandara knows of your eagerness to help. If they need you, they will come for you."

"How will they get a message to me through this?"

"Nandara knows to use the dragons. She summoned them before. You've never seen them do it, but they will bend their customs to the point of breaking when it's required."

Neesha kept her gaze fixed out into the rain, looking past her mother and out toward a city lost to the grey deluge. She hadn't had much time to talk to Nandara before the rains had come and trapped her at the farm. All she could do was hope Nandara would call on her.

Neesha was miserably soaked in the rain, warm at least against the body of the dragoness, but soaked nonetheless and with nothing dry or clean to wear once they landed. Nandara hadn't provided specifics when she summoned Neesha to the city, but it must important if the dragons were ferrying her over the flooded plain. The prospect of meeting other Guild wizards made Neesha grin.

Some of the houses zipping past below, the ones in lower-lying areas, were submerged up to their roofs. Neesha's home, at least, was on a gentle knoll and safe from the waters so far, their cold cellar muddy but not deluged. At least, not yet. Their neighbours had lost their barn and were living in their loft because the rest of the house was in ankle-deep flood waters.

The dragoness spiralled downward through the sheets of rain to the ground outside the city, setting Neesha on the road right where the cobblestones began. Neesha had hoped to be delivered straight to the hall the wizards were using, but she had not earned the same favour with the dragons that her mother had. The dragoness had brought Neesha this far only because of Dionelle.

Neesha bowed in gratitude, wanting to make sure she had a way home. "Thank you, Mistress. I'm in your debt."

The dragoness huffed hot air at her, and then disappeared in a torrent of wings and wind. Neesha shielded her eyes against the rain and made her slow way through the deep puddles toward the centre of the city, where Nandara waited for her. She began shivering not long after the dragoness was gone. Her riding cloak had done her well enough, though it didn't fasten around her belly anymore, and the hood had blown back in flight, letting water rush down her back. Trying to ignore the discomfort as much as she could, Neesha focused on reaching her destination—and warmth.

The market square was nearly deserted when she passed through. Only vendors with storage in the city had anything left to sell, and they huddled under tarps, trying to keep their wares from getting drenched. She groaned internally when she saw Stone at one of the tables, selling baked goods with another vendor she didn't recognize.

"Neesha!" He pulled up his hood and came out to join her. "I wouldn't have expected to see you in from the fields."

"A dragon brought me." She didn't stop. Her voice was clipped. She didn't want to dance around the usual awkwardness, hoped he would leave her to continue on her way. Instead, he fell in stride beside her.

"Ah yes, they would to help your mother, wouldn't they? Wish I had one to take me home!"

Neesha shot him a look. "Are you trapped in the city?"

"Aye. The roads are under water nearly as tall as I am. I came in before it got too bad. There are a few of us here from the outer fields who didn't have the sense to leave before the roads washed away. So here we sit."

"I'm sorry to hear that. I will likely be staying with Nandara for a time. I have some wizarding to do, it would seem."

"Ah, it's serious work that's brought you into the city."

"I doubt Nandara would summon dragons to fetch me if it wasn't something important."

"Shall I walk you to your destination?"

She wanted to say no, but he was always kind to her in the face of her incessant rejection. And if she slipped in the water, she would certainly need his help.

"Thank you, Stone."

They trudged silently through the everlasting downpour, the only sound from the rain and the mud squelching beneath their feet. Neesha had expected awkwardness and was surprised by how comfortable the silence was. But her boots were full of water, and she wondered if she would ever be truly dry again. They finally reached the hall at the edge of the royal grounds where Nandara and the others waited for her.

"Thank you again, Stone. I hope the waters recede soon and you can return home." A thought struck her then. "Stone, where are your children?"

She couldn't be certain in the gloom, but it seemed like his face lost some of its colour before he squared himself.

"They're home with my mother."

Something like a cold brick settled in Neesha's gut. His children were his entire world—something she was beginning to understand. Stone had been widowed and lost his third child in the same day. It was the only reason she had initially held back her cruelty. She didn't want to imagine what it must be like for him, separated from them, awash in uncertainty.

"Well, best I get in there and see if I can't help them do something about all this water—get you back to them quickly."

Stone took her hand and bowed over it, hiding his expression from her. His hand was warm around hers, a steadying comfort. A solid presence. She felt certain his need for her was borne out of more than convenience. There was emotion behind it. Deep but deliberate.

And she was young and sturdy and a powerful wizard. Did he hope she would be someone to rely on, especially in a crisis where he currently had only his aging mother for aid?

No wonder he sought her out. Nothing could heal his wound, it was far too great, but having Neesha at his side could provide a balm, could make the pain something he could bear. There was no knowing yet what kind of mother she would be—to her own child or someone else's—but she wasn't a monster. His children would always be safe with her.

Knowing what she meant to him didn't bring her any closer to understanding what he could be for her, what need he could fill. He was ten years her senior with all the knowledge and security it brought, but if she gained entry to the Guild, she'd have all the security she needed. She would not be with the man for pity's sake. Neither of them deserved that.

Stone smiled at her, small and a little sad. He glanced at the door.

"I'd best not keep you. Be safe, m'dear," he said, dropping her hand. Then he turned and disappeared back into the gloom.

Neesha watched the wall of water swallow him and shivered. She wanted to call after him, to tell him he was the one who needed to stay safe. Shaking her head at her own foolishness, she turned her attention to what had brought her out into such miserable weather.

The entrance hall was warm, if damp, and sheltered from the rain hammering down on the roof. Steam rose off Neesha's chilled skin and soggy clothing, and she was surprised and relieved by the suddenness with which the sensation of pelting droplets ceased once she was indoors.

"Neesha?" Nandara called from farther in the building. She appeared at the head of the nearby hallway, looking troubled. "Come quickly, they're ready to begin."

"I'm soaked," Neesha said.

"So is the whole of Pasdale. The fire is warm, you will dry quickly enough, now come on."

Neesha scowled and followed Nandara down the long hallway, relieved that the entire building was made of stone. The farmhouse had begun to take on water. It soaked through the wood, making everything damper and the house creaked unnaturally as the wood expanded. The stone building held the heat far better and Neesha was pleased at least for the change of scenery, even if she was stuck in wet clothes.

The end of the hallway opened into a large domed chamber, its many skylights revealing the anemic daylight beyond. The room was largely lit by lamplight and a blazing fire in a massive hearth that nearly spanned the wall at the head of the room. There were tables arranged in concentric circles, but they had been pushed back so that the gathered wizards stood in the middle. Some of the older ones sat at the tables nearest the centre of the room. There were a dozen of them exactly, fourteen with Neesha and Nandara, and it was far too silent for a room that held so many people.

Some of them were preparing to speak, but Neesha walked right through the middle of the group and straight to the fire. She pulled off her damp boots, tipping them upside down and resting them at the edge of the hearth, close enough to dry quickly, but not close enough to burn. She stripped off her riding cloak and hung it over a chair near the fire and wrung out her hair.

"Are you quite ready?" one of them asked her.

"If someone wants to explain what this is about, I'm listening," Neesha said tersely. "But I'm sure you notice I cannot afford illness right now."

Not caring what they thought, she stripped off her clothes down to her britches and squeezed out as much water as she could before wriggling back into her damp garments. Nandara, the only one really used to her ways, wasn't fazed by her actions and explained while the others uncomfortably averted their gazes.

"We're going to give you your exams today," Nandara said.

Neesha stopped in the middle of wringing out her shirt and looked up, startled.

"You said I wasn't ready!"

Neesha protested the decision but turned back toward the fire, feigning a need for its warmth to hide her grin. Her mind buzzed and she itched to call her power forward and let them see what she could do. Maybe she could even call a demon for them. She stretched her mind to recall if it was sanctioned. Maybe she'd have to wait until she passed.

"I think you might be ready enough. I just didn't want to risk it," Nandara said. "But we need all the pyromancers we can get."

"It's that bad, is it?" Neesha asked.

There had to be a reason Nandara had finally agreed to the exam, after all this time and what it meant to Neesha. Suddenly, she almost wished she was back at the soggy farmhouse, safe from the danger, wrapped quietly in peace. She shivered, though she wasn't entirely convinced it was from the cold. She wanted to crawl into the fireplace and stay there.

"We've been able to confirm our suspicions that water demons are involved," Nandara said. "Draxli appears to have recruited some aquamancers to his cause, though we have no scouts to confirm any details for us. One thing we do know is that they are using water demons to bring intense flooding rains to everything in their path. It's not only that." Nandara glanced around at the others gathered before returning her gaze to Neesha. "They've got monsters of the seas—large ocean snakes that travel up the flooded rivers all the way from their mouths. The dragons have confirmed that Draxli's forces are following waterways for this purpose."

Neesha stopped. She couldn't move or think or speak. No wonder dragons were dying. Would the demonfire she'd been secretly learning to use help?

"What do we do?" Neesha asked.

"We start by seeing if you're ready to assist us," Nandara said. "Your mother told me what you did with the fire demon—how you can wield a measure of control over them." Nandara gave her a stern look. "Dangerous and foolish. But the Guild is willing to overlook you stepping so far beyond the bounds of apprenticeship for now. Today, we will see if you're prepared enough to meet the Guild's demands."

Neesha remained by the fire, too cold and damp to move away from it yet, regardless of what was expected of her. It was difficult to keep her composure, even around so many sombre wizards. People who would soon be her colleagues. She didn't want to seem over eager, but it was no secret how desperately she yearned for this.

Just as she considered risking illness and moving from the fire to join them, they moved from the centre of the room and took seats closer to the fire. Nandara stood off to the side, explaining that she was merely there to observe. Normally, Nandara would have been giving the exam on her own. Things were far from normal.

The exam opened with a verbal test pertaining to the theory of spellcraft. The gathered Guild practitioners took turns posing questions to her. Some of them she knew immediately, many of them she had to guess. There were very few of them she didn't know at all. She managed not to grin as she answered. Had Nandara really been so worried about this?

It had been late morning when she'd arrived in the hall, and once the first part of her exam was complete, they broke for lunch, Nandara bringing Neesha a bowl of thick, hearty stew, perfect for such a chilling day. Neesha's clothing was mostly dry by the time the second portion of her exam began. When the group reconvened, there were ingredients and tools of spellcraft set out on the table near the fire. Neesha was instructed to make certain basic potions—pain salves to aid healing, mind balms to ease terrors, tonics to promote strength, acids to melt weapons and rocks. These were probably Neesha's biggest weakness, but all of her final products worked, even if most of them were weak.

She wasn't concerned because she knew what was left. When they called on her to wield actual spells, she did so with a wide grin. Most of it was basic: simple energy transfers, small object levitation, basic elemental spells. These were things she'd been doing since she was a child. Things she could do in her sleep. The Guild practitioners gave her some more advanced tests in elemental magic, most of it in pyromancy.

Searing fire coursed through her, warming her like nothing ever could, and performing pyromancy so consumed her that the exam and the gathered wizards and the rain fell away for a while. In that moment, she was living fire.

They had her call up a fire demon. This gave her pause. Was it a test? Not of her skill but her character? She glanced at Nandara who waved her on.

Neesha stood in front of the fire, arms open as if to embrace it, and effortlessly spoke the words Nandara had so many times. Words Neesha had had far more practice with than any apprentice had a right to.

The demon arrived in a flash, a spot of light brighter than the rest of the fire, and Neesha took a steadying breath, holding her focus. Using the language she'd been taught, Neesha held it under control, keeping it at the edge of the hearth with barely a thought.

Neesha turned to the other wizards, grinning, certain they had to be impressed. Most of them were bent together, talking softly, but the oldest woman there, sitting alone at the end of a bench, shook her head and stood. Leaning on a cane, she came a few steps closer, fixated on the demon behind Neesha.

"Foolish. You know that?" she asked.

"Yes." Neesha barely managed to be modest. "But at the pace we were practicing..." Neesha glanced at Nandara. "It was so painfully slow. With fire... I just had to try it."

The woman pinched her mouth into a puckered little line, so tight it nearly vanished. She watched the demon.

"Foolish. Dangerous," she said, looking at Neesha. "Remarkable control, however."

Then the woman turned back to the others and bent into the conversation.

"I can wield its power," Neesha said.

"Yes, we have heard."

"I can show you."

"We believe your mistress."

Neesha recognized the dismissal in the tone. She released the demon, pushing it back into its own realm, and stood near the fire, watching the rest of them deliberate and struggling not to grin like a fool. There was no way they could keep her out of the Guild after all that. She'd done better than in any of her practice tests with Nandara. And the old wizard had clearly been impressed by Neesha's demon work.

She tried not to think that she'd get her wish after all. Admittance to the Guild before her child arrived.

Nandara sat at the edge of the tight circle the others had formed. Their voices all mingled into one muffled whisper, barely audible over the sizzle and crack of the fire. With it all out of the way and nothing to do but await their decision, the excitement died away and Neesha felt familiar aches and deep-seeded tiredness settling in. She wrapped herself in her now-dry riding cloak and curled up on the fur rug near the hearth.

Neesha had begun to doze in the shroud of warmth when she heard Nandara's voice.

"Are you certain?" Her mentor sounded distressed.

Neesha sat up as Nandara approached her, the other wizards talking quietly amongst themselves. Nandara sat next to her before Neesha stood up. The dour look on Nandara's face dropped an entire winter's worth of cold into Neesha's gut.

"It's not good enough," Nandara said softly, shaking her head.

"Ridiculous!" Neesha hissed through clenched teeth.

"There's no denying your ability as a pyromancer, but that alone isn't enough to admit you to the Guild."

"But I answered all the questions, all my potions worked! How can they say it's not good enough?"

"Nee, you are not very good at theory and your potions were terrible. Confidence is not the same as talent."

Neesha had noticed that her practice time with Nandara of late consisted primarily of focusing on the things she hated the most. She was a natural mage and hadn't needed to learn much theory in order to practice.

The things many wizards had to study for years, she had been able to do innately. How could they punish her for that?

"So that's it? I can do all the things they asked of me, but because I couldn't properly recite some useless booklore, I've lost my chance? Why would you agree to this if I wasn't ready?"

Neesha stood, heart racing and body numb, and paced, wanting to slam her fists into something. Some*one*, maybe. And to prove what fools they all were, she refrained from letting her emotions into the fire. She stuffed it down into itself rather than letting it flare.

"She has a point," Nandara said, her voice louder to carry to the Guild members pretending not to listen. "We urged her to do this before she was ready, it doesn't seem right to me to deny her. She's capable, she just needs more time."

Another of the older wizards, possibly the very oldest among them, rose from the group and shuffled closer to where Neesha paced. He was so old that Neesha wondered if he'd been around to witness the birth of the mountains surrounding Pasdale. He was withered and stooped, leaning heavily on his staff, and though his snowy white beard was not long, it nearly reached the floor. His eyes, though, were dark and alert and intelligent inside the folds of umber skin, wrinkle upon wrinkle, on his face.

"We do not have more time," he said, his voice paper thin.

"That's not my fault!"

Nandara placed a hand on Neesha's shoulder, interrupting her prowling and her shouting. Neesha couldn't stop trembling. They couldn't take her future away from her like this. She'd burn the lot of them to cinder if they tried.

Nandara's grip on her shoulder tightened and Neesha bit back her rage.

"This is about more than our current difficulties," Nandara said gently. "Pasdale may fall, despite our efforts, and we will need further aid to suppress Draxli if he reclaims a place of power."

"What do you suggest?" the old man asked.

"Ignore today's results. This exam never happened." Nandara scrutinized the man. "Let her try when she's ready—we need talent like hers. I warned you this could happen."

He ran one gnarled hand through his beard, nodding slowly, and turned away, rejoining the seated group.

Nandara maintained her hold on Neesha.

The group didn't talk for very long when he came back, a little smile folded into the wrinkles of his face.

"You may retake the exam when you're ready," he said. "We will overlook today's failure. But you must discontinue practices unsanctioned for an apprentice." He cast a meaningful glance toward the fire, as if the demon were still there.

"But what about the war?" Neesha said. "I can help! I can wield those demons and reduce Draxli's sea beasts to ash!"

"We have other powerful pyromancers," he said.

"Then why ask me to do this at all? I am fireborn, we all know what that means. There are things I can do that no one else can."

His smile returned. "That is true, lass. But you are still not ready."

"If Draxli drowns us all, what's it going to matter?"

Nandara gripped her shoulder.

"Frax," Nandara said slowly, thoughtfully, addressing the old man. "What about temporary admittance for her? These are desperate times and they call for extraordinary measures. We asked her here because we need what she can do. I will remain by her side at all times, guide her in all ways. But she's right, we need her."

His gnarled fingers were back in his beard. "She outperforms exactly where we need her to. Temporary admittance?"

Neesha felt lightheaded. Was there still a chance?

"There's precedent for it," Nandara said. "Temporary entrance to the Guild, conditional on her helping defeat Draxli. Lasting only as long as it takes to turn his forces away. Then she goes back to her studies and takes the exam properly, when she's ready."

He gave a fractional nod and went back to the others, bending into the whispers. This time, they took an eternity. Sometimes things got heated enough for a hissed whisper to ring through the room, but never heated enough that Neesha actually understood them. She was rooted to the spot, numbly watching the group.

At last, the old wizard got up. Neesha held her breath and went utterly still.

He smiled. "You did well enough—particularly in the area we most need your aid—that we have agreed to grant you an emergency temporary entrance to the Guild. It will last as long as the war does. But you are not to use magic above your station without your mentor present."

Neesha closed her eyes and let out a long breath.

"Thank you, Frax," Nandara said.

"No, no. You are correct. We must not waste talent, particularly not in times of need."

Neesha kept her exuberance to herself. It was her surprise she expressed freely.

"Just like that?" she asked. "I thought there were documents to be presented, and that measures like this would take months to pass. It took a fortnight just to grant amnesty to Ondias when the Dunhams nearly killed her out of their own stupidity. How is this possible so quickly?"

The old man quirked an unsettlingly bushy eyebrow at Nandara.

"Neesha, this is Grand Chancellor Fraxnir, head of our Guild," Nandara said. "Not as many wizards as we would have liked were able to make it, but he was and so were a few others of the Guild's high council. Enough that they have the power to pass instant emergency decisions."

Neesha had no idea what the customs were. In normal circumstances, she would have received word of her entrance remotely and with plenty of time to prepare for formalities before the official welcome and introduction to the Guild. So she bowed gratefully, just as she had with Lady Zyx.

"Now we get to work," Nandara said.

Neesha pressed her lips together and joined the other wizards as they made their plans to oppose Draxli.

CHAPTER NINE

Swirling dark clouds towered over the valley of Pasdale, a wall of water obscuring the city and fields. The storm roiled in place, stationary above the valley. From Neesha's vantage point in the mountains, she should have been able to see for leagues, but it was nothing but water all around.

She shivered despite the warmth of her cloak and clenched her jaw against rising bile. Her imagination failed her as she tried to envision the kind of conflagration required to dispel this much water. And what kind of effect would that have on the city?

Neesha stood between her mother and Nandara at the edge of the line of wizards gathered at the crest of the hill, a steep drop to the valley before them.

There was a persistent drizzle where they waited but nothing like the deluge below. Still, the rain ended entirely not far from where they stood, and the dragons had already gathered the wood they would need to begin their defense. It rapidly dampened in the rain they faced, but remained dry enough that it wouldn't stand against dragonfire. Or Neesha's power.

She wasn't certain what her role would be—perhaps little more than a guide for the flames once the fire was set. But there might also be so much more. If the plan failed, the dragons would be relying on her. Neesha would turn to her last resort. None of Nandara's warnings changed what she could do—what she'd have to do, if there was nothing else. After all this time, Neesha couldn't imagine it would cause more harm, if it had done anything to the babe at all.

A twinge of guilt tried to settle into her gut, but Neesha was too excited about the prospect of further proving herself. She itched to use pyromancy, to push the boundaries of her abilities.

Nandara was a mistress of the elements, able to control them all, and she was preparing the groundwork for a spell to urge a return to balance in the elements. An aquamancer stood with them, not a powerful man, but one well versed in his area of focus. He guided Nandara in the process, lending his wisdom to her power.

First they would try to restore order in a subtle manner, encouraging the water demons to release their grip and let nature do the rest. Should that fail, Nandara would call a water demon forth from a barrel of rainwater they had brought with them and try to negotiate with the creature. Failing that, they would begin countermeasures involving fire and air. That was where Neesha's talents, guided by Nandara, would be most useful, though some of the other wizards would be harnessing each other's power to amplify the effect. She knew only that it was possible, but not what it entailed, as it was a skill for master level wizards. She buzzed at the prospect of doing what she had always dreamed of—working as a true elemental wizard—but ice settled in her veins at the thought of them needing to resort to her skills.

Clashing elements could be disastrous. If Neesha heated the water but failed to vaporize it, a boiling deluge could cook the city's inhabitants. Nandara would oversee the team of aeromancers tasked with pushing steam away from the city once the pyromancers started their work, but no one had tried anything on this scale before, and the extent of Neesha's power and control was largely untested.

While Neesha and the other elementals worked their spells, some of the other wizards, including the Grand Chancellor, monitored the storm and demon activity.

These were all things far beyond Neesha's reckoning. She would need years of study to understand and perform spells of this magnitude and requiring such finesse. She stood wrapped in her firecloak, stamping her feet, waiting to see if she would be needed. The entire blaze of dragons from the surrounding mountain ranges plus some of their allies stood in a line behind the wizards. Eight dragons in total—allied with Pasdale through longstanding accords that her mother had helped shore up.

There was a new dragoness with them, an emerald and scarlet one Neesha had seen when Draxli's storms had first come to Pasdale. She was sister to the grey and scarlet dragon of Pasdale's blaze and the leader of the nearest blaze of allies, one that had already lost two dragons to Draxli's efforts.

The dragons had brought the group of wizards and their supplies out to the edge of the storm, waiting to see if their aid would be further needed. Like Neesha, they would be involved in a countermeasure using fire to combat the water demons' influence. If the dragons became involved, the plan was to call upon enough fire demons to possess each of the dragons, which would exponentially increase the power of their dragonfire. Fire demons possessing dragons posed less risk than a fire demon possessing Neesha. Dragons themselves were very much like pyromancers, but with a closer relationship to fire demons and their realm.

The black dragoness lay with her head between Dionelle and Neesha, watching the spells closely, while the others sat back, awaiting her command.

"Will this work?" Neesha asked.

The dragoness snorted doubtfully but watched on.

"The water demons have been focused on the dragons," Dionelle said. "Whoever is controlling them is unlikely to relinquish their grip, despite any threats we make."

"We'll have to use fire, won't we?"

"I think so. We need to end this quickly."

Neesha looked grimly northward, knowing Draxli's forces were mere days away from them. Lady Zyx had officially declared war and sent a request for support to Golden Hill. Still, the battle would have come to them before any aid—even the swiftly moving dragons—made it to them. They would be largely on their own, though neighbouring blazes of dragons, like the emerald and scarlet's, had pledged their support. There were two dozen additional dragons within a two-day flight of Pasdale.

Nandara stopped her spellcasting and looked to the Grand Chancellor, who only shook his head grimly. Nandara immediately bent over the rain barrel and did a quick summoning, as Neesha had seen her do so many times before. The response from the water demons was instant. Nandara's negotiations were made too quietly for Neesha to hear, and much of what she said was spoken in the spell language that the elements were most receptive to. Neesha only understood the language of fire demons.

Neesha startled when Nandara cried out and recoiled from the barrel, the water rising up in a furious funnel, lashing out at her. The dragoness lifted her head above the humans and shot a huge blast of fire at the water and the barrel containing it, joined in by the other dragoness. Their combined efforts vaporized the water, leaving the water demon with too little to work with to remain a threat.

Neesha stood motionless through it all, her breath caught in her chest. She'd reached for her pyromancy, her hands tingling with power, when the dragonesses reacted. Neesha remained taut.

"They will move their storms toward us. We must act now," Nandara said, standing once again. Her voice was tight and her words clipped with urgency.

A warm rush filled Neesha, her pulse quickening and her skin tingling as she called up her power. She leaned forward, intent on Nandara, waiting for instruction.

The pair of dragonesses blasted the stack of wood into a massive bonfire as the storm moved their way, the wall of water shifting and growing as it approached them. Cold fear froze Neesha's veins. But she maintained her focus on Nandara and the fire.

"Neesha, we will certainly need your aid," Nandara said.

Neesha met Nandara's gaze, her eyes widening. Already? They needed her already? She nodded and turned her full attention on the fire.

"We need demons in the dragons immediately," Nandara instructed. "Then we need to do as much as we can with the fire we've got. We've got to stop their advance, gather more fire energy, and unleash an assault on the storm."

Demons in dragons. Stop the advance.

Neesha moved closer to the bonfire, cool and numb despite its heat, and pulled her cloak tighter to protect her clothing. She held out her hand, physically pulling flames from the fire and cupping a tiny blaze.

Her mother and Nandara moved closer, Nandara cringing against the heat. All three of them summoned fire demons, Neesha doing it from the fire in her hands, one that had grown to nearly her own size. It grew bigger, flaring in brightness as a demon appeared before her.

A spike of heat throbbed down her spine.

She wouldn't keep this demon for herself. The instant it appeared, she grinned but released it, using her will to push it out to the dragons who circled tightly overhead.

With the three women working, three voices in unison, they quickly had three demons, and then three more. It took barely a heartbeat to fill the eight dragons with fire. The demons responded not only to the pyromancers, who were like kin to them, but also to the summons inviting them to battle other elements.

Neesha smiled, smug and satisfied, but refrained from looking at the Guild wizards. It was hard not to grin like a fool, she felt so light. If they noticed how well she'd done, they'd *have* to change their minds about the temporary nature of her admittance to the Guild.

She looked out over the valley where the possessed dragons circled high above the clouds, beyond the influence of the water. They rained fire down on the storm, a terrifying blaze cascading against the water and boiling it away. The aeromancers channelled great gusts of wind, funnelling the scalding steam northward out of the valley and toward Draxli's position.

A wicked smile spread across Neesha's face.

She pulled at the flame, tremendous heat pouring through her body. With a gesture, she cast the fire away from her, through a gap in the line of wizards, so that it cascaded down the mountain. A firefall.

More demons appeared as Nandara and Dionelle summoned them. Neesha drew on their influence and coupled it with her own skills.

The fire cascading down the hillside tumbled over itself, growing more intense. It burned nearly white hot, heating the air until the water could no longer be sustained. A great roar rose up around her as so much water vaporized. The fire consumed the trees and shrubs along the slope as it moved, compounding the power Neesha poured into it.

Nandara and Dionelle worked with her, pushing the fire to rapidly consume what lay before it and stopping the wall of water a mere half-league from where they worked, boiling it away. With the aid of the aeromancers' gale, they pushed the fire northward at an impossible pace.

Neesha grinned as the fire circled the valley to cut the storm off from its supply—the river flowing to the northern mountains. The river was dammed where it entered the valley in the south, and the dragons had already taken a team of Lady Zyx's people out there to begin cutting off the flow of water.

Now the fire raged toward the dam, as unnaturally quick as the storm had moved, to make a barrier of heat too great for the water to penetrate. Neesha's breath quickened. It was working!

"It's not enough!" Nandara called, somewhere on the other side of the firefall Neesha poured down the mountainside.

What did she mean? The storm was cut off.

And then she saw.

The storm was shrinking, but intensifying, its fury concentrated directly over Pasdale. The deluge worsened. Neesha thought she saw steam rising from the city.

"Oh gods," she muttered. There wasn't enough fire to vaporize it instantly, not enough wind to move it off the city.

The dragons worked in unison, concentrating their fire where it mattered. Still, it wasn't enough. That was her city, dammit. She'd be charred before she'd let anyone drown it.

Numbing heat coursed through her as Neesha dug deep into herself, deep into the fire, no doubt reaching all the way into the fire realm, and threw all of her might into sending power to the flames. The response was immediate. She felt nothing but the rushing flame and could barely see through the brightness.

Still she grinned. She was powerful woman who deserved a place in the Guild.

Her body barely held itself up. But the fire did the job for her. Was she inside the fire? It was so bright she couldn't tell.

She squinted into the valley, focusing on where she needed to drive the flames. She pulled from the once tiny bonfire, pulled directly from the dragons themselves. With a determined push of will, she drove bonfire and dragonflame alike out over the valley.

A great conflagration of dragonflame and demonfire grew into a rolling fireball consuming all the sky and boiling away the rain.

Neesha set her jaw against fatigue, squinting against the growing brightness, pulling more flame. She was a goddess burning like the sun itself, her exhausted body buoyed by the warmth.

The fire rushed passed her, and she heard nothing but the crackling and hissing of flame, not even the roar of steam rising into the gale. The heat through her body soothed her so that she wondered how she'd ever doubted their success. Her success.

Of course she'd be a Guild member. A permanent one. Not that she worried. Not when she had so much fire. Why should she worry when surrounded by this power? Fire was all she needed. She floated in it, at peace, and closed her eyes.

But suddenly she sank, dragged down to some great depths.

"Neesha!" Nandara screamed.

Neesha jolted. The blazing light around her seared her vision, and she scrunched her eyes closed against it as absolute darkness rose up to claim her.

CHAPTER TEN

R eiser only half-listened to Dionelle's explanation of the impending battle, his wife's words lost amid his concerns over the encroaching water. The cold storage rooms in both houses had already flooded, and with much more rain, they would have to start living upstairs. And he knew they were the fortunate ones, that some people had lost their entire homes already, that others had died. Even as he sheltered under the front veranda, the spray from the downpour had soaked him through in the few minutes he'd been outside. The raindrops stampeded over the tile roof, their rumbling course muffled within walls but nearly deafening outside.

Dionelle's hand on his jaw brought him back to the present.

"Don't fret, love," she said softly. "We will stop the rain. We'll stop it today."

He didn't doubt her words, but even without knowing the specific plan, he was aware of the dangers. It involved Neesha and the dragons and other powerful wizards. He'd overheard Sharice and Dionelle fretting over Neesha's newest trick with demons, and while it seemed like a useful tactic given the circumstances, that kind of power did not belong with a girl like Neesha. Dionelle seemed confident, but Reiser had so many concerns.

That Neesha hadn't fully passed her entrance exams was a new concern. It was clear that her magic was the only thing she really cared about, so her failure meant there was something deeply wrong. It troubled him because he knew how much the plan relied on her. He couldn't see what had changed that made Dionelle put so much trust in the girl.

He'd feel better if she stayed behind. He wished he could go with Dionelle instead. All those years ago, Reiser had failed to protect Dionelle from Draxli's wrath. He hated to stand by a second time. But he was no courtier, no wizard, certainly no warrior, and in his heart, he did not want to be.

Yet it felt wrong that he could not protect those he loved.

Dionelle turned from him as the black dragoness dropped soundlessly out of the sky—even the sound of her great body slapping down into the sodden fields surrounding them couldn't compete with the monstrous din of the rain.

Neesha stood silently apart from them, her face turned out toward the rain. It wasn't unusual for her to go out of her way to keep from meeting his gaze. She wordlessly walked out into the rain to meet the dragoness, and Reiser turned back to Dionelle.

"It will be all right. She's taking this seriously."

"That doesn't mean she's capable of handling the responsibility," he said. "And she clearly doesn't have all the skills she needs."

"And that's why there will be others there. Fraxnir himself will be overseeing everything, and Nandara will help watch her. My power is no match for this," Dionelle said, a touch of sadness to her voice. "I'm going primarily to watch over Neesha."

The dragoness huffed impatiently and Reiser desperately grabbed Dionelle's arm.

"We can't delay," Dionelle said. "I will come back to you. She'll see to it."

They both glanced to the dragoness, and she huffed out a brief streamer of fire, hissing through the rain. The dragoness had never let them down before, but something about this felt different. He couldn't shake his desire to go with them. Still, he knew he couldn't keep them from the battle, nor could he go with them—he'd only be in the way. He kissed Dionelle quickly and held her briefly, then he let her join Neesha and the dragoness.

It was troubling how quickly they vanished into the rain. Reiser retreated back into the house, where Sharice waited with the boys. She'd made the dangerous trek from the old farmhouse across the quagmire of the yard to join them in waiting for news. Reiser hadn't seen much of his mother-in-law since the rain began, and he was sad for that, but someone had to stay with Neesha. It was a small price for not having to see nearly so much of the girl. Having her and that expanding stomach of hers on the front porch with Dionelle had been difficult enough.

Conversation died when Reiser entered the house, so he knew they'd been talking about Neesha. His scowl intensified as he stripped off his soggy boots and cloak and squelched across the parlour to the hearth, rifling through the embers with the poker, stirring up more heat and flame. He placed two more logs on the fire and fanned it, only scowling deeper as he realized he could never produce a flame large enough to fully push back the chill and the dampness caused by the unending rain.

Reiser only resented Dionelle's absence that much more. He'd overheard Sharice comment that Neesha had been able to do the same, to drive back the dampness in the front room, but it was something the girl was able to sustain so long as the fire burned. And of course, with a Joasera woman in each house—a pyromancer each—the fires rarely went out in either home, even in the sweltering depths of summer.

Despite the dampness, the tiles around the hearth were warm, and Reiser welcomed the heat on his clammy skin. He sat back and let the fire dry his clothing. With two natural pyromancers in the house—fireborn, as Dionelle had first referred to her condition after Neesha's birth—all that stone had become a necessity. He sighed wearily, Neesha weighing heavily on him today.

"That babe is going to be fireborn," he said.

The silence only deepened and at the edge of his vision he noticed Bly and Breen exchanging a quick glance while Sharice only watched him curiously. He'd never spoken of the child before, but there was no way he could deny it much longer. He turned back to the hearth, glowering. Trying not to think that his wife's life was in the hands of such a careless girl.

He wondered if Stone's home lived up to the man's name. He wished the man himself lived up to the name and wasn't so soft. Reiser had considered carting Neesha off to Stone's farm and leaving her there, grace of the monks or not. Stone would never have it, of course. Neesha had to go there willingly, and so far as Reiser could tell, the girl hadn't willingly done a wise thing in her life. He only hoped the child's arrival would force some sense into the girl.

"Mamma says Neesha's baby is going to be even more powerful," Breen piped up.

"And more weird," Bly said.

Reiser glanced at the boys and nodded wearily. He'd tried not to give it much thought, but it made sense, all things considered. Especially with Neesha tampering with the elements in ways she wasn't meant to.

"And just think of everything the baby will be able to do," Sharice said softly, a touch of excitement in her voice. "Neesha's power has been far beyond anything Di was ever capable of."

Reiser sighed, wishing he hadn't brought it up. He had no desire at all to talk about the child or his daughter. He stood abruptly and walked to the front of the house, facing west. Dionelle told him they were going to the western slopes, getting beyond the rain, to do what they had to.

He was alarmed to see that the water level burbled at the top step of the porch. It had risen even since he'd last been out, minutes ago. It already lapped over the stones and would be at the doorway by the afternoon. He looked further out into the eternal gloom, wondering if he'd be able to see any of the spellcraft, wondering how he'd know if it had worked. The only part of the plan that he'd really paid attention to, that he really understood, was that the effort would initially focus on forcing nature back into balance. Fire was the last resort.

The silence in the room softened and the boys sassed each other as only brothers could. Reiser didn't like when his moods darkened the home. The tension was difficult to bear, too much like when he'd nearly lost Dionelle so early in their marriage. It was another reason he tried not to think about Neesha and what she'd done.

Sharice joined him at the window, watching quietly for a time.

"You're going to have to come to terms with it. Soon. You know that," she said.

"She can stay with you," Reiser said tersely. "There's no reason for me to be involved."

He paused, trying not to think of where they may have gone wrong with the girl.

"It will be different once the child is here," he continued. "If it doesn't have the same devil in it as Neesha, if Di's good standing helps us weather the scandal with dignity, it may still go well for all of us."

Sharice sighed but held her silence.

None of them wanted to talk about what would happen if things did not go well. There had been many lengthy arguments about it already, but Dionelle had relented, saying that if Neesha's indiscretions continued to hurt the family, the baby could stay but Neesha would be turned out. Sharice had balked at the idea—it was too close to what had happened to Vyranna. If it came to that, Reiser only hoped that the girl would find her way better than her aunt had.

"If their first attempts to end the rain work, will it end all at once?" Reiser asked. "Has Dionelle told you?"

Sharice stared out the window. "She wasn't certain, but said that there wasn't much they could do that would end the rain immediately. The rain will let up, even if it takes some time for the storm to continue on its natural course. If it works, we should have proper sunlight tomorrow."

"And if they use fire?"

She looked toward the hearth and took so long to answer that Reiser didn't think she would.

"Then may the spirits bless us all."

Reiser stood up straighter. Her lips were pinched shut and her brows furrowed as she glanced out the window, looking west.

"They'll try to boil the water out of the sky. If it doesn't vaporize, the water left above us will come down super-heated."

Reiser shuddered. At least there wouldn't be many people outside to suffer boiling rain, if that's what it came to. But would it matter?

Reiser remained at the window in a silent vigil with Sharice while the boys remained near the hearth. He couldn't stop worrying about Dionelle. Every shift in the rain turned his thoughts back to her. She was far out of her depth, left to rely on the dragons and a girl who had proven time and again that she could not be trusted.

As much as he hated their plan, he had been soft with his objections and left it alone after that. Meddling in the affairs of dragons and wizards had nearly cost him his soulmate, and he knew well enough to stay out of Dionelle's business. He worried nonetheless. His growing sense of dread made him wish he'd been more forceful this time—that he'd let the dragoness cart off Neesha and left Dionelle where she belonged. Dionelle had never used fire to combat another element before. She had never been trained to do so.

The rain lashed the house with renewed force, startling Reiser and Sharice away from the window. Sharice stayed back, but Reiser stepped forward again, his face nearly pressed against the glass as he watched the gloom darken and take shape in the west. Seized by fear, he realized that the rain and the storm had solidified into a wall of water—a towering spout gathering itself to assail the western slopes.

"Sweet spirits, be with them," he breathed.

Reiser dashed to the front door, throwing it open and sloshing through the water inundating the porch. He stood near the railing, squinting to see more. There was a faint glow to the west, but at such a distance, he feared he imagined it. Sharice and the boys came to the doorway, but none of them ventured beyond the threshold. Then the storm shifted enough to obscure his view of the glow, if it had ever really been there.

He stood rooted to the spot, unable to look away. His thoughts locked onto his wife in silent prayer for her safety. He had begun to tremble when a volley of lights erupted across the sky in the west, the flashes spreading out in all directions. Each burst illuminated a patch of sky, briefly parting the clouds before the gloom closed in and swallowed up the natural light.

"That must be the dragons," Sharice said.

Still watching, feeling the first tinge of hope since the rain began, Reiser nodded dumbly.

But his limbs quickly grew cold. The dragonfire wasn't going to be enough on its own, that much was obvious. They would need all of the dragons of the realm, not only the Pasdale blaze, to vaporize a storm of this magnitude.

But then the glow returned like a confused sun rising in the west, but this was no ball of fire. It was a long, glowing stream spreading like arms in a welcoming embrace, reaching to encircle the valley and stretching rapidly to the north. Toward the threat.

Reiser trembled. He remembered then that Dionelle had mentioned something about cutting off the rain's supply. They were reaching out with an unparalleled blaze to strike down their enemies in the northern passes.

Reiser's hope coalesced as Sharice joined him, resting a tentative hand on his shoulder.

"It just might work," she whispered, her voice thick with hope.

The boys were busy cheering on their mother and their sister, unconcerned with the dangers. Then an even greater light, roaring like thunder, erupted from the point in the west where it all began. Reiser's hopes jolted back into fear, a cold buzz on his skin, as he watched the light spread over the entire valley. It rumbled toward them, a great conflagration sweeping across the sky, hissing like a million dragons as an entire storm evaporated explosively.

A near-forgotten memory of the fire realm rose to the surface of his mind like a malicious ghost, and his knees buckled. It sounded so much like the speech of fire demons and like the hiss of the unreal fires of their realm.

Sharice cried out behind him, her footsteps retreating into the house, but he could do little more than raise his arms in front of his face to block out the blinding light and protect against any boiling rainwater that might escape. The light was so bright that he feared it would consume everything in its path, scorching the valley right down to the bedrock, reducing them all to ash.

The noise roared passed him and echoed out of existence, steamy warmth caressing his face and thickening the air. The silence that followed was absolute—Reiser's breathing and scrape of feet across wood the only sound—but the blazing light remained. Reiser feared the entire valley had been lit ablaze.

"Oh, blessed spirits, they did it," Sharice said from behind him, her voice a thin whisper choked by emotion.

Reiser opened his eyes and lowered his arms, squinting against the brightness, against the sun's blazing reflection off the surface of the stilling floodwaters. Shielding his eyes against the glare, he looked up to see the sky hazy but clear of everything except eight dragons, all rushing back toward the western slopes.

Sharice and the boys retreated back into the house, shutting the door behind them.

Even though the saturated air was difficult to breathe, Reiser remained outside, leaning on the porch railing and watching the west as mist rose all around him. He watched the western mountains and waited. The dragons would bring Dionelle home now. Surely there couldn't be anything left for them to do.

The dragons rose into the air, one by one, with five of them heading northward and two disappearing back over the western slope. A moment later, a final dragon rose up from the foothills, swooping directly back toward the city. Reiser tromped across the sodden porch, following the dragon's trajectory. The air had cleared enough for him to see she was black as the depths of despair.

Delivering news to Lady Zyx? he wondered. *Is Dionelle with her?*

He gripped the railing and watched the city. It had been difficult from the start, but when the wall of water had made its way toward the western slopes, unease had settled in his heart. The longer Dionelle was away, the tighter uncertainty's grip. There was a lot he couldn't forgive Neesha for, but if she had botched a spell through defiance or her usual careless inattention, he wouldn't wait for the babe to arrive before turning the girl out. He was ready to wash his hands of her.

He hadn't heard Sharice come out and startled at the touch of her hand on his arm. He half-turned to face her.

"It's all right now," she said gently.

"The water's gone but we don't know for certain that it's all right until Dionelle comes home." He looked back toward Pasdale. "I can't lose her again."

"I know you're worried about Neesha making things worse, but she's no match for that dragoness."

Reiser nodded, trying to take comfort in that knowledge. Neesha could still only wield fire and that couldn't hurt the dragons. It could hurt Dionelle—she felt the pain of it even if it didn't cause tangible damage—and that could cause different kinds of injuries. The girl had already inflicted enough of those on the entire family.

He had watched Dionelle suffer enough at the hands of Vyranna long before Neesha became aware of the kind of devastating emotional power she held. If something had gone wrong this time, if Neesha was to blame for further grief, he would not hold back his wrath.

Reiser leaned on the railing, shifting his weight to relieve the ache in his legs. Sharice had periodically joined his vigil over the course of the afternoon, but she had just gone back in, leaving him standing alone at the corner of the porch. The sun edged passed its zenith, burning away the lingering water vapour in the air. Gentle waves lapped at the edge of the porch, the floodwaters slowly receding.

And yet Reiser couldn't leave his post. Not until Dionelle returned. A simple report to Lady Zyx shouldn't have taken so long, and the fact that the dragoness hadn't left the city yet was troubling.

A dull ache had settled in behind his eyes when the dragoness's large shape lifted out of the city centre and angled toward his homestead. He tensed and moved to the top of the stairs, waiting. A moment before she dropped into the water in front of him, he realized that she was alone.

"Mistress!" he called. "Where is Dionelle?"

The dragoness leaned forward and arched her long neck so that her face loomed in front of him.

"Forgive me, rancher," she said. "I do not wish to lie in the muck as we converse."

Reiser nodded and waved her on, encouraging her to drop the formalities.

"Neesha is unwell and Dionelle will not leave her side."

"Dionelle is unharmed?"

"She is quite well. However, she insists on staying in the city until Neesha is well enough to return home."

"Thank you for delivering the news, Mistress." The sun's warmth, hidden for so many days, finally reached the heart of him. He gave the dragoness a thankful bow and then watched on politely, waiting for her to take leave of him. But she tilted her head and gave him a reproachful look.

"Neesha was remarkable," the dragoness said. "She opened a portal to the fire realm and poured trueflame into the storm."

Reiser shuddered, remembering the hiss of fire scouring the sky.

"It took dragons and wizards combined to wield it, but had she not opened that gate, we would have been doomed. She did well today, but was unprepared for the taxing nature of the spellcraft. The healer is uncertain about her condition, but the girl seems simply asleep to my eyes."

He bowed his head to hide his face from the keen judgement in the dragoness's eyes. He knew better than to manufacture concern he didn't feel, knew the consequences of being false with a dragon. Still, she expected something of him. If nothing else, he could show his relief and gratitude that Neesha hadn't gotten his wife killed. Smiling, he straightened.

"Thank you for this news, Mistress. I am truly surprised by Neesha's contribution."

The dragoness smiled, a brief upturn of her vast mouth. "Your daughter is alive with mystery, and she has only just begun."

That's what I'm afraid of.

Reiser did not voice his thoughts, hoping silently that a sense of responsibility would accompany the expansion of her power.

The dragoness gave a nod and then lifted herself to her full height, backing away. Knowing exactly the mess her wings would churn up as she departed, Reiser didn't hesitate before moving back inside where Sharice and the boys waited to hear the news. He didn't go to his family, not right away. Instead he stood at the window, speckled with fresh mud as the dragoness took flight, and watched her depart for the city where his wife kept vigil over their daughter.

He was certainly grateful that the girl had ended the water siege. Perhaps even a touch proud of the achievement. Perhaps Neesha saving the city would give that very city cause to overlook her indiscretions. It would go a long way to helping him learn to mend the rift between him and his daughter. But he was a long measure from forgiveness.

CHAPTER ELEVEN

S unlight seared Neesha's eyes through her eyelids, and she squinted hard to peek through her eyelashes at the world beyond. After so much gloom and rain, then crushing darkness, the sunlight was welcome, even if she couldn't cope with it yet. She closed her eyes. Waited.

It was quiet, wherever she was. No footsteps or voices, no birdsong or clatter of city dwellers. No sound of rainfall. It was warm and dry. Somewhere soft.

Neesha felt heavy, as though she could sink into marble like it was feathers. She fought her eyelids open, the bright light less painful now. There was a window next to her, shutters thrown open, and she could see the rooftops of the city, spreading on forever. She was in a tower. Possibly in the palace. The span of city beyond her certainly suggested the centre of Pasdale, though she wasn't used to seeing it from this height.

Neesha shifted her head, a monumental effort, trying to get a better look out the window. She tried sitting up but may as well have been trying to push over a mountain. So she shifted her head the other way, taking in the room. It was small, the walls and floor made of stone. Just her bed, a chair and short table next to it. The table and chair both stood empty at the moment. The door leading out into a bright marble hallway stood open.

Still, not a sound.

She remembered nothing since being given temporary entrance to the Guild. But she remembered that war loomed. She finally called out. What had meant to be a shout—a demand for aid and answers—squeaked out as the barest whisper. The sound stirred someone nearby and a woman in crisp robes the calming blue of healing suddenly appeared in the doorway.

"Ah, there you are. Out of the darkness, finally."

There *had* been darkness, cold and consuming. Neesha frowned. Where had the dark come from? It wasn't like sleep. She couldn't remember any dreams and certainly didn't feel rested.

But the healer smiled at Neesha, and all of Neesha's fears melted away.

"You'll want to see your mother, I'm sure," the woman said. "I'll let her know you're awake. But I'll need to examine you first, now that you can answer some of my questions."

Neesha scowled, impatience rising, as the woman asked her foolish things like her name and age and when she expected the baby to arrive. How long had Neesha been in the dark? The flutter of the baby cartwheeling in her stomach suggested it hadn't been very long.

The healer prodded her, asking if anything hurt. Nothing did, but Neesha couldn't move her leaden limbs. She'd never felt so profoundly tired.

"It will take you quite some time to recover your strength, I'm afraid," the healer said, her tone touched by remorse. "As I understand it, you're lucky to be alive. Left your mentor with quite a challenge."

Nandara! When had she last seen her? Cold panic gave Neesha the strength to lift her head. She recalled her mentor recoiling from a barrel of water demons. Like water bursting a dam, memories of the battle against the rain came flooding back, though she couldn't remember what had happened that would bring her to a healer's care.

Before Neesha could force any questions from her lips, the healer had vanished from sight. The sound of a door clicking shut left her in silence. Neesha drifted in and out of troubled sleep, dreaming of fire and steam and of drowning, and awoke to her mother's face hovering over her. Dionelle smiled when Neesha opened her eyes.

"You were not ready for such an undertaking." Dionelle's tone was soft, but reverent. Her mouth smiled but her eyes were sad. "You did remarkably well despite that."

Dionelle stroked her cheek, the sensation warming Neesha in a strange and familiar way. Dionelle and Neesha, stoked by powerful internal fires, were always warm, feeling feverish to those around them, making the touch of others always seem cold. It was a rare occurrence when the touch of another felt anything but frigid against Neesha's ever-burning skin. Though Dionelle's fires had diminished since she long ago renounced the demon essence in her, enough had remained, bound with her very life force, that her skin was still as hot as Neesha's.

But Neesha couldn't remember the last time her mother had been gentle with her. Or the last time Dionelle had shown concern. Whatever personal tectonic shift had caused this, Neesha had missed it.

"Mamma," Neesha said, hoarse and barely able to speak. "Happened?"

Dionelle pursed her lips and held a cup of water to Neesha's mouth. Lifting her head, even a little, even for a couple of sips, was exhausting. Dionelle set the cup aside and looked out the window.

"None of us are entirely certain what happened," she said, meeting Neesha's gaze. "You nearly died."

She already knew that much from the healer.

"Rain?" Neesha asked.

Dionelle blinked. "Vaporized." Her voice was soft as she spoke, full of wonder. "Took only a few minutes for whatever you did to blanket the entire valley in fire. It was magnificent. And terrifying."

"Dragons?"

"They're well. All of them. They secured victory for us and chased back Draxli's forces once your fire cleared the storm. Do you remember what you did? Or how you did it?"

"Fire realm," Neesha said, not entirely sure what she meant.

Dionelle stilled and stared straight ahead with sightless eyes. At last, she shifted her gaze back to Neesha and swallowed.

"Yes, it was very much like the fire realm. It even sounded like the fire realm. Do you think you drew power directly from there?"

Neesha twitched one shoulder, unable to remember much from those final moments. She remembered being angry and afraid, she remembered how powerful and awesome the dragons had been with demon aid, and she remembered standing between Nandara and her mother in front of a bonfire. She had no recollection of anything she had done. Maybe she'd taken possession of a demon by accident.

Dionelle smiled, but it still didn't reach her eyes. "I'm sure more will come to you as you recover your strength. Once you start wielding fire again, it will open up new paths to memory and the spells will reveal themselves."

"Nandara?" Neesha asked.

"She has been working with other elementals to uncover what happened with that fire of yours." A bright sheen of tears welled up in Dionelle's eyes, and she blinked rapidly against them. "Nandara broke whatever enchantment it was that has taken so much out of you."

Dionelle looked toward the door. "But Healer Irina insists you need rest and I've got so much work to do with all the blazes of dragons arriving. We drove off Draxli's water for now, but it will return and we must be ready. You rest. In another day or two you can return home."

Enchantment? That didn't make any sense. Nor did it make sense that pyromancy would exhaust her so deeply. Neesha opened her mouth, trying to force words through her parched lips, but Dionelle kissed her forehead, her lips like a tender fever. Then she was gone, and Healer Irina immediately appeared next to her.

"What...?" Neesha croaked.

"Hush now, dear one. Your questions will be answered in time."

The healer helped Neesha sit up more and tipped a saucer of broth to her lips. In her confusion, Neesha had missed her hunger, but the taste of even simple broth left her ravenous. As the broth soothed her need, questions bubbled back to the surface of her mind.

"How did—"

"I don't have the answers you seek," the healer said. "I know only what your mother has said. Now, you need rest. Trust that you are safe—you will heal faster without your worries."

Neesha settled back onto the mountain of pillows while the healer left her with the cup of water at her bedside. The door clicked shut and Neesha scowled. What had her mother said? The water would return. She didn't need to be lying around in bed. She needed to be with Nandara, figuring out what she'd done so she could replicate it. Safely this time. Maybe the other pyromancers could too. A whole group of them wielding that kind of fire would surely end Draxli for good.

Bracing her arms, Neesha tried to push herself to sitting, but it was like she'd been melded to the bed. She growled in wordless frustration and lay back, trying to remember more of what had happened. She needed to be ready when Draxli returned. How much time did she have? Days? Weeks?

The baby churned in her stomach, a reminder of how precarious time was.

Neesha breathed deeply and closed her eyes, resigned to the bedrest. For now. But the battle would return and she would be ready.

CHAPTER TWELVE

There was no great hall where Draxli could entertain the dragons out in the wildlands, but that suited him just fine. These particular beasts shunned the pomp of their kin, foolish niceties Draxli had little patience for. Beasts had no place making demands. This mountain plateau was adequate for the purpose, giving him view of his forces in the valley below.

More to the point, the whole camp saw him convening with beasts that would gladly devour most of them on sight. Draxli kept his smile in check.

A great golden dragoness stood before him on the mountainside, and she needed no meddling whisperer to converse with him. She was the largest dragoness he had ever seen, and her splendour led her to believe she ought to be one of the Superiors. Her grievances meant little to him, though he couldn't argue her pure majesty. One such as her was born to lead, and she was here because he had promised that she would.

"We've lost one of our own," she said gravely.

He glanced at her when she spoke but saw that she stared pointedly out over the mountain range, sitting on her haunches. A corner of his mouth curled upward. He continued surveying his camp.

"There are always risks in war. You have done well not to lose any in your staged raids to the east. A commendable effort that has greatly advanced our cause."

He smiled magnanimously with the slightest of bows. These beasts loved flattery. That should soften the way. He stood straighter.

"We will proceed as planned, and Loch can destroy them once our forces are closer. He's a young lad, still gaining mastery of his craft. A plight made more arduous by the fact that his mentors have abandoned him."

The dragoness narrowed her eyes at him. "He will have greater power nearer to the city?"

"His power is great, but limited by the distance. We do not have the time to wait for him to gain the mastery he needs. Zyx is wise to us, and we must continue the assault on Pasdale to keep her from seeing our true target."

The dragoness snarled. "But if the boy can't drown Pasdale from here, how will he take down the dragon city?"

Draxli gave her a wry look. "The boy isn't my only aquamancer. Have faith, my friend! He is overseeing the onslaught on Pasdale, but I have others, more experienced, who will be leading the attack on the dragon city. They will channel his power when the time comes. They are working in tandem, expanding their abilities."

Draxli looked out over the camp below him in the valley and was pleased by how impeccable Loch's timing was as a monstrous water vortex rose up out of the river, just ahead of the fragile fleet carrying his forces. It had taken careful planning to ensure that the aquamancers' training session coincided with the dragon visit.

"Ah, there they go. You see? Their skills grow each day. The dragon city will be yours by the end of the next moon." He gestured expansively and turned back to the dragoness, smiling broadly. "This recent battle was little more than practice for them."

"And what of the defeat we suffered?"

"You think it was a defeat?" Draxli asked good-naturedly. "I am quite saddened to hear that you lost a comrade. We suffered some losses as well, but we know our enemies' weak points. We must target the fireborn girl quickly next time, and then we will have little to fear."

Draxli smiled at the thought. Yes, the wizards had certainly shown their hand in battle, but if his forces struck again before the wizards had time to gather more of their own force, overpowering them would be simple. Draxli simply needed to concentrate his aquamancers and drown the foolish pup—hopefully her mother as well. With that dreadful fireborn family laid to waste, Draxli could easily reclaim Pasdale and restore it to its former glory. It pained him to see how the great city had been sullied by his cousin's piteously soft heart.

The vortex over the river continued to rise and widen, spewing out a furious storm, much like the one they had recently unleashed on Pasdale. It billowed out over the valley and the dragoness suddenly hissed. Her male companion cried out in alarm. Squinting, Draxli saw a sky blue shape against the grey of the clouds.

The dragoness called for an attack, but the blue dragon was already making a quick retreat, and once beyond the cloud range, he would be difficult to trace. Draxli scowled, rage pounding through his veins, but he kept his voice calm when he spoke.

"Pay him no heed," Draxli said. "His warning will not reach the city in time."

"If the Superiors are prepared for the attack, they will hold the city."

How could such a magnificent creature need so much coddling? How could something so bloodthirsty have such a short memory for victory?

"They will drown. The city will be yours. You saw the deluge upstream," Draxli said, recalling how quickly they had inundated the valley, wiping out the last of Zyx's allies who stood in their way. A smile touched his lips, drawing one corner up.

The dragon spy had soured his mood, but his forces had always been prepared to move quickly. He would have liked more time, but swift action gave his enemies less opportunity to plan countermeasures. No, this was not ideal, but it would not be a problem.

He glanced up at the beast in front of him, hoping she was through voicing her concerns for the moment. At least there were only four of them left to deal with. He wondered briefly what would become of the traitorous dragons once the fire demons discovered the extent of their betrayal. The thought was fleeting. If they died in battle, that would save him having to deal with them. If they succeeded but did not remain loyal to him, he would drown them with the rest of their kind.

He turned back to the camp, where the vortex's peak consumed the whole of the sky with no end to the storm clouds roiling overhead.

"The attack on Pasdale," the dragoness said. "How will that stop the Wizards Guild or the king from retaliating?"

Draxli scoffed. She really was a daft beast, wasn't she?

"By the time the king's forces can make it to Pasdale from Golden Hill, the whole of the valley will be our stronghold. Without those fireborn women standing in our way, the city will fall quickly—willingly, even. And the wizards? They take even longer than dragons to get through their ridiculous formalities and decide upon anything. With the dragon city gone, they will not stand against us."

"That intimidation will only last so long."

"Yes, my friend, but it is certainly not the end of my plans." He gave her his winningest smile. "Remember, we have done well—particularly with your help—to portray dragon sympathizing in a poor light. I do not think the king and the wizards will find allies in this cause for long."

With the pyromancers focused on his attack on Pasdale, they would miss the larger battle. Speed was necessary, but the attack was already well under way. Even if he failed now, the raids had planted the seeds of discontent he needed. Victory would be his. It was only a matter of when.

CHAPTER THIRTEEN

It was cool for late summer, and Neesha pulled her cloak tighter around her as she settled into the wagon, preparing for the long ride through the valley. As much as she didn't want to leave the warm comfort of the healer's tower at the edge of the palace, it would be nice to get home. Neesha just wasn't interested in the part where she had to be out of bed to get there. And then there was the long climb up to her room once she was home.

She reclined, propped on cushions in the back of the wagon while her mother steered it over the city's cobblestones. Keeping her eyes closed, she tried to ignore the vibrations shuddering up through the wheels. If only the dragons would deliver her home the way they'd delivered her to the healer. She'd be warmer clutched against a dragon, and the trip would be faster and smoother.

After four days under Healer Irina's care, Neesha was still exhausted and now she was irritable too. The inaction weighed on her. A steady rotation of dragons guarded the valley with concentrated efforts to the north. More wizards had arrived from the Guild, now that the water had receded and the roads were passable again. She should be doing more than lying around in the back of a wagon.

As desperately as she wanted to help, there was no denying that rest was what she needed. This inner conflict bred perpetual frustration that was only exacerbated by the miserable trip. The comfort of being home, at least, would be a welcome change.

Neesha had finally adjusted to the wagon's rhythm and was teetering along the edge of sleep when the wagon halted. Growling out her irritation,

Neesha opened her eyes and looked around. That was when she heard Nandara's voice.

"Di! A moment!"

Neesha sighed. She'd been desperate to hear from Nandara as she lay in the tower. Now that she was on her way home, she only wanted to get to her bed. She sat up straighter and picked her mentor out of the crowd. Nandara drew up next the wagon not long after it stopped.

"Everything all right?" Dionelle asked.

"I meant to stop in earlier today, but I've been preoccupied with the new envoy of Guild wizards arriving. I just got word you were taking Neesha home. She's feeling well?"

Nandara glanced to Neesha as she asked it. Neesha shrugged.

"She's on her feet again, but exhausted," Dionelle said. "She still doesn't remember anything."

"I haven't learned anything from the other elementals." Nandara met Neesha's gaze, her mouth pinched shut. "Even with dragons and demons involved, with the strongest pyromancers in the Guild, we couldn't replicate anything even close to that firestorm. What you said about the fire realm makes sense. It's the only thing we can think of. It seems likely that you opened a direct link to the fire realm."

Neesha had suspected that much for days.

"That doesn't explain why I'm so tired. The fire realm energized Mamma when she was there."

"But only while I was there," Dionelle said. "I was weak and tired when I returned."

It had taken the whole of the dragon court to send her father to the fire realm after her mother so many years before, so Neesha couldn't see how one novice elemental could open a direct link to the realm, fireborn or not.

"Still doesn't make sense."

Nandara shared a look with Dionelle.

"What?" Neesha scowled. "What happened after it all went dark?"

"There were fire demons, more than we'd called up," Nandara said. "I initially thought you had died wielding that fire and pushed the demons back into their realm so I could reach you. When I did that, the quality of the fire changed. And something about you changed as well. You came back." Nandara's gaze drew inward and she shook her head.

"Came back from where? I thought I was in that fire all along."

"Your body certainly was," Nandara said, her voice so quiet Neesha barely heard her.

Neesha felt cold, like a worm slithered up her spine. A sense of engulfing darkness lurked at the edge of memory. Neesha forced herself to think of how bright and warm the fire had been. She remembered only vague flashes of it, of incredible power buoying her, making her feel bigger than a dragon. And the cold dark lingered like hoarfrost on a spring morning.

She turned away from Nandara and huddled deeper into her nest of cushions.

"I need to get her home," Dionelle said, a touch of apology.

"I'll come by when she's got some energy, see if we can understand it better. But next time you're in the city, seek me out. We have more to discuss."

Dionelle got the wagon moving again. Neesha had no doubt that Draxli and his floods were what the two women needed to talk about. They'd pushed him back but hadn't stopped him. And her mother had alluded to him using more than water to fight the battle. There were rumours about the dragons, but Dionelle hadn't specified yet. Neesha hoped to find out more now that she was strong enough to go home.

The rumble of the wagon over stone had just began lulling Neesha back to sleep when they left the city. The rutted dirt track beyond Pasdale's cobblestone streets jolted the wagon and jarred Neesha back to full wakefulness. She grumbled wordlessly, tried to get comfortable, and nudged up against sleep several more times on the way home. Unfortunately, each would-be nap was thwarted by another jarring bump in the road.

When the wagon halted at the homestead, Neesha sank into the cushions with relief. She remained there, watching the pale grey sky while she waited for her mother to get her grandmother. It would take them both to get her out of the wagon. She hoped she wouldn't suffer the indignity of one or both of her brothers being fetched to lift her out.

The thought helped her find enough energy to sit up and pull herself to the edge. Dionelle and Sharice came out quickly, one on each side to help ease her down. It seemed like leagues to the porch. As much as Neesha wanted to curl up into her bed and sleep for a week, she suspected the sofa in front of the hearth would have to do.

Her mother and grandmother still on either side of her, they started the slow shuffle toward the house. They'd barely made it halfway from the wagon when the black dragoness, glimmering and sleek as always, came down from the sky and landed in the field beyond the farmhouse.

She approached carefully, always cautious around the homesteads, not wanting to startle anyone or stumble onto anything she shouldn't. She came to the front porch, lying out across the whole of their yard, her head resting at the foot of the stairs that the two older women helped Neesha toward.

"Does she remember yet?" the dragoness asked Dionelle.

"Nothing more, Mistress."

"May I speak with her?"

"As you wish. Sharice and I will prepare her room for her while you talk."

Neesha held the railing and stood at the bottom of the stairs, facing the massive dragoness. Neesha was tall enough to see over her snout and look her in her gleaming obsidian eyes.

"How may I serve you?" Neesha asked, well enough to remember the bare minimum of her manners. She did nothing to hide her exhaustion. Hopefully this would be quick.

The dragoness narrowed her eyes. The world lit up in roaring bright intensity and Neesha cried out, throwing her arms in front of her. Without the railing for support, and with the blast hitting her square in the face, she toppled backward into the dragoness's large outstretched hand.

"What in the name of the moons is wrong with you?" Neesha snapped, forgetting niceties.

The dragoness harrumphed at her and steadied her on her feet, studying her closely.

"You were afraid," the dragoness said. "Why?"

"You were trying to light me on fire!"

"Nonsense. I know you would never burn. Why would you fear fire now, after a lifetime of benefit from it? You should fear fire no more than you should fear rain or wind."

"I am in no condition to suffer your riddles," Neesha said.

"I am the one suffering riddles," the dragoness said, but her tone was light. "Your very being has been a riddle since the day you were born. And that fire you called forth was unlike anything I have ever seen."

This stopped Neesha on the first step, and she turned to the great beast before her.

"Fire is your life," Neesha said. "How have you never seen such a thing before?"

"How, indeed. I favour Nandara's speculation, but that doesn't explain why you would now be afraid of a flame."

The dragoness shot her with flame again—this time it was a slow fireball, one less startling, but Neesha flinched, even with time to see it coming. It didn't hit her with any kind of force, and it didn't hurt at all, as it never had. Neesha realized that the dragoness was taking care to aim the fire at Neesha's head, keeping it away from her clothing.

It was a thoughtful gesture, but Neesha would rather not be the focus of experiments right this moment.

"Mistress, I have no doubt that you're fascinated by this. I am curious about the answers as well, but I am purely exhausted. May we continue this when I am feeling more myself?"

"In a moment, my dear," the dragoness said. "I am going to try one more time. I want you to recall as much of the battle as you can and hold it in your mind. I want you to open your eyes while the flame consumes your vision and tell me if you remember anything more."

Neesha sighed wearily and gripped the railing, turning to face the dragoness wholly. She closed her eyes against the brightness at first, and then opened them, squinting fiercely against the intensity while she thought of the bonfire on the hill. And then she remembered what had been so terrifying.

"A voice," she called out, startled at the memory. Despite the warmth of the dragoness's flames, cold prickled across her skin. "A terrible voice in a language I couldn't understand. It was in the flames."

The dragoness ceased the flame and watched her closely.

"Did the voice hiss? Like some great serpent or water sizzling against a burning log?"

"Yes. It was terrible. Like the fire demons when we call them, but also not. I've never felt threatened by the demons I've worked with. And I can understand them. This was different."

"It was a demon speaking to you in its native tongue. What you think of as their language, what you speak when you work with them, it is a poor translation. They use their own tongue within their realm and use only the common elemental tongue when conversing with humans in this realm. I would love to know what it said to you, but I don't expect you can repeat any of it."

"I didn't understand any of it."

"But they were speaking to you. Nandara was right."

Neesha's eyes widened in shock, and she collapsed against the stairs, tingling pain shooting up her backside and through her body.

"And that is why you are so profoundly exhausted," the dragoness said. "A mere human is not meant to open the way from this world to their realm. I wonder, then, just how much more demon essence is in you. Certainly more than we expected."

No wonder Neesha had felt so powerful that dragons were mere insects in comparison. And if she'd opened a way between the worlds once, she could certainly do it again. The prospect was exciting, but she felt cold.

"And my child? Stronger than me just as I am stronger than my mother?"

"That possibility exists. Particularly after all that has happened. We will have our answer before the next moon. Get your rest."

The dragoness stood then and trotted back out into the open field before leaping into the air, her large feet leaving craters in the soft earth where she had pushed off. The gale of her wings was strong against Neesha's face even from such a distance. Then she silently disappeared out toward the horizon and into the mountains to continue her patrol.

Neesha let out a shaky breath and realized only when she reached for the railing to stand that she'd had both arms wrapped protectively around her belly. Having answers hadn't offered her the comfort she'd hoped for. The comfort of the sofa, at least, didn't let her down. With Sharice's help, she settled in and sank swiftly into sleep.

Neesha finished her soup and set the bowl on the low table in front of the sofa. She wrapped her blankets around her and settled back into the cushions. Her mother and grandmother had recently left for the market to pick up supplies Dionelle hadn't been able to when bringing Neesha home that morning. With Sharice gone and the boys working until dusk, Neesha could rest undisturbed.

As much as her mother had insisted she sleep, Neesha's naps had been frequently interrupted.

The fire was high and warm as she curled under her blankets. She started to relax, the warmth seeping into her, when someone knocked at the door.

Neesha growled and dug deeper into the blankets. The knock came again. Struggling up out of her cozy little haven, Neesha swore under her breath and started for the door. She thought that it was someone in the family, but why would any of them bother to knock?

When she flung back the door, she could only stand in the threshold, blinking back confusion.

"I'm sorry to bother you," Stone said. "Talk of what you did with that fire made its way around the market, and I wanted to be certain you're all right."

She nodded and stepped out onto the porch to join him.

"I'm sure my mother could have told you that and saved you the trip."

"It's not your mother I wanted to speak to."

Neesha crossed her arms around herself and scrutinized him.

"What's brought you all the way out here that couldn't wait?"

Leaning against the support post, he held her gaze. Neesha almost heard the gears spinning in his head.

"I know you've been quick to reject your mother's attempts to match us," he said haltingly. Neesha hated the hurt in his voice. "I wish you'd reconsider."

She shook her head and looked out into the lane that led back to the city.

"Then forget your mother's meddling and consider the proposal fresh. Consider it as my own, a true request of you. Not something contrived out of your family's desperation."

Neesha had never heard him speak so eloquently and wondered if maybe he wasn't as slow as she'd always believed. She gave him a quick glance and shook her head.

"Please hear me," he said. "This isn't as you believe. Hear my intentions."

She wanted him to go, her body screaming out for those cozy blankets she'd left behind. But she couldn't bring herself to slam the door in his face. She didn't look back at him, but nodded, once, quickly, and then led him into the house. He sat next to her on the sofa, each of them turned slightly so that they faced each other, but she curled up in her little nest of cushions, just out of reach.

"I don't know what you hope to accomplish," she said.

"Please, just hear me."

She bit her lips and stared at the fire.

"Neesha, I know what you think of me, and I know you don't love me."

She sucked a breath through her teeth. His words bit into her, and she turned her head completely, facing the other way and squeezing her eyes closed for a moment. He kept talking.

"I don't need you to love me as I love you. I simply want to be part of your life, for you to be part of mine."

She shook her head and looked at him. "No. I can't do that just because you're lonely and I, allegedly, need a husband." She sighed, too tired to summon the curt words she needed to get him back out the door. "You're a good man, Stone. You deserve a woman who loves you in return."

He shook his head. "Few matches are based on love. Your parents were lucky, but everyone else learns it along the way. I don't need a woman who loves me, no matter what you think I deserve. I want you for your companionship and the joy it brings me to see you. I want to help you for no other reason than that. You need the help—you'll need it very soon."

"And so I should just take your offer?" She tried to keep the anger out of her voice. He glanced at the fire when it rose at her words but didn't comment on it. "Whether I think the offer is right? I should take it just because it's there? Because you're the only one desperate enough to want me?"

Stone sighed and focused on her carefully.

"Nee, if I had met you before wedding Talienna, I would have broken our match and sought you instead. I want you not out of desperation. My want is true. I would treat your babe as one of my own."

"And I suppose you expect me to treat River and Ember as mine?" Her voice simmered at the edge of anger.

"That would be for you and the children to decide." He spread his hands palm up in a helpless gesture. "My mother provides all the care they need. She would resist our match at first, but she's a good woman and she would accept your child all the same."

Neesha considered his words instead of outright rejecting them as she always had. It sounded like a good deal—but that was the problem. She didn't want a deal. She didn't want to take the offer because she had to.

"I know that things are difficult with your father," Stone said. "I know they will continue to be. Whether he will soften once the babe arrives is a matter to be seen, but do you want to take that risk? You're going to need help. I'm offering you stability, Neesha. Am I truly worse than being turned out into the street?"

"Of course not," she snapped, the fire flaring. "But I want the decision to be my own, not a coercion."

"I don't mean to tame you, only to offer you a solid foundation." He watched her, waiting for her to look at him. She looked away from the fire and met his gaze. "I know how much pyromancy means to you, that magic is the only thing truly your own. I wouldn't dream of interfering in that. Your little one will, at least for a time, but that's temporary and any support you let me offer you will only bring you what you desire that much quicker."

"I can be independent on my own," Neesha said. "Breen overheard my parents talking. It's likely they'll turn me out, but keep my babe here. That seems best for all of us. I'm sure Nandara will let me stay with her until I can support myself."

Something dark passed through Stone's expression. "You would cast your child aside so easily? Just walk away?"

"I'm sure my family will do a much better job than I ever could."

"Hurl abuse at me all it pleases you," he said, his tone rising, "but do not dismiss your own child."

"Who are you to tell me what to do?"

"Who are you to shun the precious gift you have?"

The muscles across her chest and shoulders tightened and hot rage settled in her stomach. "This is not—"

Before she could say the pregnancy was no gift but a curse and a burden, she remembered exactly what Stone had been through. Why he was a widower. She snapped her mouth shut, swallowed back her hot anger.

"This isn't your concern. I don't need your help."

Stone's expression softened and became pitying. She hated to see it, was so tired of that look everywhere she went, and she wanted to rage against whatever words he had next. At first he didn't say a thing. He leaned closer to her, resting a hand over her belly, the other hand rested on her shoulder.

"A mother's way is never easy," he said gently. He slid his arm all the way around her shoulder and leaned his forehead against hers.

Neesha held her breath, ready to push him away.

He continued to speak softly. "Talienna knew it, lamented it often. I'm sure if you asked your mother or your grandmother they would say the same. Being married didn't change it for them even if it eased the way. Becoming a mother changes expectations. Let me ease your burden."

Neesha was struck by how close his words were to her mother's. She didn't want to believe them now as she had ignored them then.

She tried to cling to his words, to make sense of them, but his closeness was stifling. She shook him off and extricated herself from his embrace. Neesha moved to the hearth and paced.

But she had to give it thought, and the baby spun inside her, the movement bubbling across the taut skin of her stomach and giving her something to focus on. She knew the arrangement was a good one, knew Stone meant every word he'd said. She would have to live through the guilt of not returning his adoration, at least to start, and she tried to imagine what it would be like to eventually grow fond of him.

Will it really be that bad?

He'd shouted a moment ago. He'd gotten truly angry with her, had finally stood up to her. In the moment, all she'd wanted to do was slap him. But now she half wanted to goad him into another argument. For so long she'd feared him to be a docile coward. At least he'd proved that wrong. She needed someone who could argue with her. Not all of her spitefulness was a mask to separate her from her mother.

Neesha didn't want to admit the truth in her mother's words—didn't want to think that she'd lost herself beneath all the spiteful decisions and recklessness. She didn't want to settle.

The baby spun and Neesha stopped pacing in front of the fire, staring deep into the flames.

A tired little voice in the back of her mind tried to insist she could do it on her own. It saw all the ways her aunt had gone wrong so many years before and was convinced she could do better. But that voice was too tired to put up much fight, and Neesha was too tired to really listen anymore.

Impending motherhood wasn't leaving her much choice. She wasn't going to change society, not from the outside. And she could always get a divorce if it was awful. Her mother would *love* that. Laughter tried to burble up at the thought, and she held her breath until it passed.

But that was the whole problem, wasn't it? She didn't *want* to.

"Do you not find it insufferably wrong that I don't really have a choice in this?" She faced him.

"I can't say I've thought much on it. I suppose it's not fair."

"It's beyond fairness, Stone. It's *wrong*." She planted her feet, arms crossed in front of her and stared him down. "Who I am—who my mother is—our power, it has nothing to do with the men we marry or the children we bear. We have our own worth. *I* have *my* own worth. I shouldn't have to do this just to be allowed to use the power I have to better our world."

He stood, hands out in a placating gesture. "All right, you've got a point, but that's not how the world works."

"And what have you done lately to change how the world works? Standing here pressuring me into a marriage I don't want sure seems like a lot of the same old, doesn't it?"

He opened his mouth, closed it.

"You get what you want out of this, but what about me? What I want doesn't even come into consideration. Have you advocated at all for what I really want? Out in the market when they whisper about me, how do you respond?"

He blinked. "I... Well, I suppose I've always told the gossips it's none of our business."

She sighed. "That's an interesting start." She took a fortifying breath. "I will marry you on one condition: you help me take these expectations down from the inside. Once we're married, you're going to hear out in the market an awful lot of comments about how it's about time someone tamed me. And you're going to put those people to rights, for a start."

"That's... Being contrary isn't good for business."

"Neither is having a furious wife. Stone, you have the best produce in the valley, I don't think you have to worry about business. If you want me as your wife, this is what it takes."

"I'm but one person."

"Yes, and in this relationship you're the one with the social power. I can't change how the world sees me—how it sees other women who don't want and shouldn't need a husband. Don't you want better for Ember? Haven't you thought about what she might want when she's grown?"

"I... yes, some thought, but mayhaps not enough." He nodded slowly, looking inward.

"You're a pillar of the community, Stone. Maybe not one of the nobles or courtiers, but you've still got a lot of sway."

He looked at her. "All right, I'll see what I can do. You'll have to keep giving me suggestions, I think."

"As long as you're open to them. So we have an agreement? You help me change minds and support me in my efforts to be a Guild wizard."

"And if I do, you'll be my wife?" His voice was barely a whisper, his tone thick with confusion and softened by fear.

"After. Draxli needs to be dealt with first. But yes. I'll be your wife. I'll try."

Stone let out a long breath, all the air going out of him, and yet he seemed to grow. His presence filled the room. He took her in his arms, and she went willingly, touch-starved after so much tension with her family.

"Can we keep this between us? At least until Draxli has been dealt with?" she asked.

"Yes, of course, whatever you need. Do think of mentioning it to your mother though?"

She sighed and he smiled, touching her cheek.

"You need rest and I suppose I've got the market to manage and some gossips to set right."

She smiled and curled back into her blanket nest, allowing him to tuck her in, before watching him go. Part of her tried to be angry for giving in like this. But the rest of her was far too tired to care. She had much bigger things to worry about in the immediate future.

CHAPTER FOURTEEN

Five days after Neesha had come home from the tower, she was still exhausted, convinced she would feel drained for the rest of her days. The healer's apprentice came in to check on her every morning. The midwife came by regularly as well, now that the babe's arrival was imminent. Everything appeared normal with the child. It hadn't suffered any detectable injuries from Neesha's draining spellcraft.

She was fully mobile, but she tired quickly and climbing the stairs to her room was like climbing a mountain. She owed some of this lethargy to her growing child, but most of it was the result of the battle against the water. She was able to work on spellcraft, but that was something she could only do in very small intervals.

The spellcraft was difficult and physically taxing, something it had never been before. She probably shouldn't have been trying when she was so weak, but there was too much at risk for her to be idle. Meanwhile, she had prised some difficult truths from her mother and Nandara.

Despite the victory in driving away the storm, many lives had been lost to the floods, and the firestorm itself had caused injury and possibly some deaths. The air had initially been so saturated by water vapour that it had smothered those unfortunate enough to be outdoors. Lady Zyx had been recovering from the attempt on her life, and no order had been sent warning residents to take shelter. It was only afterward, when the woman had convalesced enough to properly command, that the message had drifted through the city. By then, of course, most people had developed their own theories about the storm, ones they would be hard-pressed to give up.

After the healer's apprentice left, Neesha reclined on the front porch, wondering if she should tell her mother the truth about Stone, when the dragoness screeched out a distant warning. Neesha's heart pounded. She struggled to sit up and then worked her way from her seat to stand at the railing and search the horizon for the beast.

Dionelle ran from the main house, where Neesha could only guess what she'd been up to. She stopped in the field next to the houses where she most frequently entertained the dragons, reaching the space before the dragoness did. Neesha was surprised that the dragoness was carrying something that looked like an old wagon, the wheels removed and a long handle fixed over the top, like a large square bucket. Neesha had seen it around, but had never known its purpose.

Dionelle's conversation with the dragoness was brief this time, and then Dionelle rushed to where Neesha watched on.

"Pack, quickly," she said. "Some clothes for all weather, comforts like pillows and blankets. Waterskins. I'll make sure your grandmother helps."

Dionelle turned back toward the main house.

"Mamma, what's going on?"

"We're leaving for the dragon city as soon as we're ready. Hurry."

Neesha's mouth fell open and she couldn't think of a single word to say to her mother's retreating back. She shook herself and got moving, shuffling back into the house and making the gruelling climb up the stairs. She put a few changes of clothing into her sack, gathered up her quilt and her pillows, and went back downstairs to where Sharice was packing baskets of food and water for the journey.

Neesha set her things down and pulled some books from the shelves, mostly of spellcraft that she had been studying, though she did include the book of dragonlore that she had been ignoring since her birthday. She had just closed up her sack when both of her brothers came in through the back door and went straight to work picking up the things Sharice had already packed and bringing them outside. Breen took the pillows and blanket that Neesha had brought downstairs.

"Nanny, what if the baby comes in the wild?"

"Your mother and the dragons will help you, dear. Don't fret."

"Should I pack anything for the baby? Swaddles or clothes?"

Sharice studied Neesha's belly thoughtfully.

"Yes," she said at last. "It's a long journey and I don't know how long you will be staying."

"Do you know why we're going? Why must I travel now, like this?"

Sharice's brow furrowed. "Something has happened, or is happening. They'll need you or they wouldn't risk bringing you. You'll get more rest on the way to the city. It's a five-day flight. Bring your sack out to the wagon and I will pack some provisions to use should the baby come early."

Neesha waddled out to the field and loaded her sack into the wagon as Sharice appeared with a pack of things for the child, as well as Neesha's winter cloak.

"It gets cold up where the dragons fly, and you'll be going through the mountains, too. You'll need this."

Dionelle drew near, her arms loaded with more provisions for the lengthy trip. She loaded the wagon while Sharice helped Neesha into it. The dragoness stood nearby, watching them silently. As soon as they'd both hugged Sharice goodbye and settled the last of their things into the wagon, the dragoness took flight, snatching the handle as she swooped past before climbing into the sky.

They were soon gliding over Pasdale, descending toward the palace. Without landing, the dragoness set the wagon down in a large courtyard where Nandara waited with a pack of her own supplies. The dragoness circled the palace until Nandara was settled in, then scooped up the wagon and headed west into the mountains.

"What's happening?" Neesha asked, troubled that her mentor was joining them.

"We've been concerned these last few days that we'd not seen any renewed attacks from the water demons, and that Draxli's forces had not advanced beyond our borders," Nandara said. "The blue dragon returned yesterday with news that the dragon city is his true target right now, with the aid of some rogue dragons—likely the ones responsible for the recent raids. Our mistress returned this morning to confirm. Draxli is not with the host near us. She tracked him through the night taking a much larger and far more dangerous host west. They travel with water's speed and might, and will reach the dragon city soon. We will be lucky if we reach it first."

"They're attacking the dragon city?" Neesha balked. The very thought chilled her, but she couldn't imagine how they could harm a city in the sky. She knew the human settlement in the valley below would be destroyed, but that would be of little concern to the dragons.

"Draxli never stopped blaming the dragons for their role in his wife's death and his exile," Nandara said. "He's been brewing rhetoric all these years, slowly twisting how events were reported, always with a spin that dragons had somehow been responsible for things going wrong."

"Is that how he got such a large host?"

"He was in a place suffering a crippling drought. Draxli blamed the dragons, brought in the last of his wealth along with water demons and aquamancers and turned everything around. That's been in the last five years or so. His army has grown since, along with the word of their prosperity after having driven out the dragons and letting the water demons in."

"When the water demons tire of Draxli's game, they're going to flood his entire kingdom," Dionelle said. "The fools don't see that, of course."

"So they follow him," Nandara said. "And some of his agents have been spreading the same foolishness into Pasdale, but with a different spin. They say the recent floods were caused by dragons because their presence working so close with people is an aberration, that it angers the demons and they're fighting back."

"That's ridiculous!" Neesha snapped.

"But people are fools," Dionelle said. "And there are very few places where dragons interact so closely with humans as in Pasdale. Even if that is only because of our family. Never mind that it's been a peaceful, prosperous time these past dozen years. The dragons have protected us, and people have flourished under Lady Zyx after so many years of the Dunhams' oppression."

"Then Draxli's poison words won't be a problem," Neesha said.

The two older women shared a troubled glance before Nandara took up the narrative.

"People are miserable," she said. "Most lost their harvests—there was so much left out in the fields when the rains came and most of that has rotted or been washed away. All this with those raids fresh in their minds. They forget the long years of peace and see only the long winter ahead, fearful of starvation."

"But that was Draxli's doing."

"Yes, but his agents have been working tirelessly with his poisoned words. With Lady Zyx too injured to lead during the vital period after the rains dissipated, there was confusion as to what had happened. It gave Draxli's people the opportunity they needed. Everyone knows that wizardry drove off the rains at last, but they don't realize the role the dragons had in that. Your part is famous, overshadowing the dragons, adding to suspicion that they are to blame."

"Goatshit! Are people really so stupid?" Angry heat crawled across Neesha's skin, anger with no place to go.

"Lady Zyx is doing her best to counter the rumours, but they've firmly taken hold and people are slow to give up their opinions once they're set in them."

"How does that affect the dragon city?" Neesha glanced up at the dragoness, who seemed oblivious to their conversation.

"The attack on Pasdale was a ruse, a diversion. Something to draw attention away from Draxli's real movements while he journeyed for the dragon city. We have sent messages for aid out to all the dragons. We can only hope the message was sent out in time."

"So we're going to help the city? Just the three of us?" Neesha asked.

"No, no. There will be more Guild members. Other dragons are ferrying them in, and Ondias is there already. She left right after the rains stopped."

The fear and troubling news left Neesha drained, and she curled up in the nest of pillows and blankets on the floor of the wagon, desperately trying to get comfortable when every inch of her ached. She finally got comfortable on her back, staring up at the dragoness's gleaming underbelly and only half listening to Nandara and her mother as they made tentative plans of defense.

"Will you expect me to repeat that conflagration from before?" Neesha asked sleepily.

"It's doubtful that you will have recovered your strength by then," Nandara said. "And I would caution you against anything so strong and foolish when we are so far from the aid we would need if something were to go wrong again. We were near healers who helped sustain you, but there is little more than an apprentice out in the dragon city."

"Then why am I coming?"

"You can still call on a demon possession," Dionelle said. "There's the chance the baby will come before the next battle, and you can wield fire and demons this time."

"But what if the baby doesn't come?"

"That's for you to decide," Dionelle said carefully. "The dragons demand nothing, but we thought it wise to bring you with us so that you're available to help if you can. You'd never forgive us if we didn't."

Neesha scoffed and closed her eyes, trying not to think about it, worrying about the long journey ahead of them. She hadn't realized she'd fallen asleep until Dionelle woke her later in the day.

"We're over the Great Mountains, if you'd like to see them," she said.

Neesha had been to the dragon city as a small child, before defiance had become a way of life for her and Dionelle couldn't risk bringing her anymore. She barely remembered the journey or anything that she'd seen. Even the dragon city itself was a vague, shimmering memory, distorted and lost in the distance of time. She struggled to sit up, so exhausted that she didn't protest when her mother helped her. She shuffled carefully to the edge of the wagon, sitting against the side and watching the mountains pass beneath. She marvelled at having lived so close to them all her life and having not seen them this close up in such a long time. They looked so small from on high, and she wished they had the time to venture down into the valleys where she could marvel at their craggy heights.

"You should have something to eat." Dionelle shifted over to sit next to her.

Nandara was huddled in her winter robes in the corner, engrossed in one of her books. Dionelle had the waterskins and one of the food baskets with her. Neesha looked out over the horizon, surprised that the sun was only two hands away from the land. She was even more surprised by how much of the day had passed and yet she wasn't hungry.

She took the waterskin out of habit but only nibbled at some of the bread her mother gave her. She barely finished it when the sun sank behind the mountains and the dragoness descended to a plateau in the middle of the range, mountains stretching out as far as she could see.

"Are you going to bring us the entire way?" Neesha asked the dragoness. "That would be far too tiring, wouldn't it?"

"I will have help tomorrow," the dragoness said. "My mate will meet us before the Great Sea."

The air was cold and the women stayed huddled in their blankets, but climbed out of the wagon to rest against the dragoness, a shimmering black furnace in the diminishing light. The sky was clear, and the stars sparkled with startling clarity through the deepest darkness Neesha had ever seen.

"What were you reading?" Neesha asked Nandara as the darkness enveloped them. There was little wood to make a fire, but with the heat of the dragoness next to them, they were plenty warm.

"Trying to learn what I can about what happened to you. There have never been pyromancers with the capabilities you and your mother have. Dionelle and I tried to replicate what you did, but even with help from the dragoness we failed."

"Is there anything in the book that will help?"

"There are theories, based largely on some dangerous work studying demon behaviour and a few demon possessions of other strong elementals. There's an account of a possessed aeromancer who conjured a whirlwind so powerful it ground down mountains. The theory is that the demon used the aeromancer's power to open a gate directly into the realm."

"Mamma's been to the fire realm, so...?" Neesha looked questioningly to her mother.

"I wasn't near enough to you when you began wielding the flame to really see. And it's been so long I'm not sure if I would trust my memory to see it. I would need to see you do it again to properly evaluate the flame."

"It makes the most sense," the dragoness said. "Especially considering her reaction to fire since."

"But if she doesn't know what she did, how can she replicate it?"

"If I opened the portal on my own, then surely I could do it with a demon's assistance."

"I'm sure you could, but I still don't think you should," Nandara said. "You barely survived the feat on your own. A demon would destroy you. That aeromancer was torn apart in the process."

"But fire can't harm me," Neesha said. "I've also had some success controlling the demon during the possession."

"Neesha, it is far too dangerous," the dragoness said. "We will do what we must to protect the city, but the whole of the dragon Superiors will be on hand when we arrive. It would be beneficial for us to learn what you did and replicate the process. We have opened gateways to the fire realm in the past, but only to send and not to receive."

"I still don't remember much of that day," Neesha said. Her memory of the event had only grown muddier with time, and she wasn't sure if she should be concerned about it or not. As for the act itself, she'd done it once already, so there was no doubt in her mind that she could call on the flame again. Still, it would be nice to call it at will and gain some measure of control over it. She didn't want to be laid up for another week.

The dragoness shifted around so that she turned her head to watch Neesha huddled in at her side.

"Your memories were strengthened by fire," she said.

"Yes, Mistress, but only to a point."

"You have not been using your spells much yet. Would you like to try again?"

Neesha thought about it, but shook her head.

"Not today, not at this late hour. Perhaps tomorrow, or once we've reached the desert."

Though it had been so long since Neesha had made the trip to the dragon city, she had heard enough of the trip's account from Ondias and her mother to know what came next. They would reach the sea the next day, and then they would either fly through the night to cross it or swing south to rest on one of the islands. Then there was the swamp, then the desert, and then they would reach the expanse of the Red Mountains.

There was plenty of time for them to work on spellcraft, and Neesha found that she just needed to internalize the fact that she would likely be called upon to battle the water demons again. She hadn't fully adjusted to the fact of the trip at all. It stretched out before her, exhausting her just to think about it—not only the trip to the city, but the trip back, which was likely to be slower. The dragoness was racing to reach the city in time to save it, but a return journey would have her feeling weary and she would certainly take two days to cross the sea then.

Neesha sighed and curled into her blankets against the dragon. The night air was cool, but once all three women had settled in for the night, the dragoness draped her wing over them, trapping in more of the heat. It was as comforting as being home, and she finally embraced sleep.

When Neesha woke up, she was back in the wagon, the blue dragon carrying them, and dawn had broken a couple of hours before. She didn't remember getting into the wagon—if she had slept through someone lifting her in, or if she had awakened long enough to climb in of her own will—and wondered how she had missed so much, not even being aware of the new dragon's presence.

The black dragoness flew ahead of them, leading the way, a black spot like a distant bird flying toward the horizon. Now that Neesha was awake, she watched the dragoness, who circled back around now and then, swooping nearby to growl and chitter at her mate, speaking in a language no human understood.

At midday, they stopped at the shore of the Great Sea, where the dragons hunted and then rested, while the humans ate and took in the view. Neesha had forgotten how impressive the ocean was, how flat the horizon became, something even the prairies hadn't prepared her for. Unending sky and water blending in the haze so that it was difficult to tell where one ended and the other began. She couldn't remember ever feeling so small.

She wondered what Stone would think of it. Would he ever leave his fields, even for a short time, to behold the sights of the dragon city and all that lay between it and Pasdale? If he truly expected her to be his wife, he'd better.

She'd like to make this trip again, under better circumstances.

"Are they going to fly through the night?" Neesha looked behind them to the dots on the mountainside that were their travel companions, resting up where the temperatures suited them better.

"They're going to try," Dionelle said. "They're going to hand the wagon off above the ocean and fly directly. If they begin to tire doing that, they'll head south to rest on a small archipelago."

"Will we make it in time?"

"It's hard to say."

It wasn't long afterward that the dragons appeared, the dragoness swooping low to pull the wagon and its riders from the beach. The dragons did fly through the night, and Neesha was jostled awake as the dragons traded the wagon in mid-air. Every time she woke, she sat near the side and looked out over the water, dizzied and disoriented as they flew through the darkness, the glitter of moons and stars shining above and reflected in glints of light on the black waters below.

Right before dawn, there was a final trade-off, and in the morning gloom she saw the distant flicker of a storm far to the south. Then the land appeared, the stinking marsh—she would never forget that smell, suddenly dreading the approach of land.

The dragons both stopped on the muddy shores, working to find a safe place to leave the wagon while they took some rest. They didn't linger in the fetid muck for long though and continued through their exhaustion, stopping only once they cleared the swamp and found dry land to rest further. With two of them, they continued through the day, taking turns carrying the humans and stopping when both dragons could no longer go forward. Once night fell, they stopped on a cool, dreary plain halfway between marsh and desert. The dragons slept with the wagon between them, their wings draped over it to protect it from the elements, while the three women slept on the ground, with Nandara and Dionelle next to the dragoness, and Neesha by herself with the male.

When morning came, she felt more refreshed, strangely re-energized despite the exhaustion of the previous day. Her body was weak and weary, but her mind was clearer than it had been in far too long. The dragoness noticed the change.

"We stop in the desert tonight," the dragoness said. "We will practice."

Neesha felt less intimidated by the prospect and hoped it was a good sign. She leafed through her spell books and even had a look at what Nandara had been reading. None of it helped jog her memory, but she felt confident about working with the dragoness once they landed. She had more of an appetite as well.

The dragons stopped more than an hour before sundown, both of them exhausted. Neesha devoured her meal and was out of the wagon quickly, pulling her firecloak around her and walking away from the others, somewhere they could work with fire and not worry about harming anything. Dionelle went with her, just to observe, and Nandara stayed put, resting near the blue dragon while she continued to study her spellbooks.

"How is this going to work?" Neesha asked.

"I will make the fire and you call forth the demon. Focus less on making the fire larger and focus instead on reaching their realm."

Neesha watched the dragoness intently as she leaned forward and blasted out flame, not for power but to consume her wholly and give her plenty to work with. The heat washed over her, relaxing her further. She knew there wasn't much time, the dragoness could only maintain that level of flame for a few moments, so Neesha immediately set to work calling forth a demon and luring it to her. Using the sparking, hissing language of the demons, she bound it to her will and held it nearby but without allowing possession.

She felt the tension in the air, sensed her mother's fear as the thing came closer, brighter than the rest of the flame surrounding her, moving with intent in a shape that was nearly cohesive. Once it was close, she persuaded it to enhance the fire and maintain the flame on its own. Then Neesha drew on its power from the blaze surrounding the two of them, trying to concentrate on the realm of fire. She recalled the fear and rage she had felt during battle, the memories flowing around her like the flames licking past, and she remembered the path she had taken, the amount of emotion she had poured into what she had done, using the demons.

She could almost taste that power again, even if she couldn't quite reach it. It made her giddy at the thought.

Flooded by the memory, she knew there was no way she could repeat the action, not in the state she was in, not without allowing the demon into her, so she called out for the dragoness to withdraw. Then she sent the demon back to its realm. The flame around them subsided.

"I can't do it without possession," Neesha growled, furious at her weakness.

"Do you remember?" Dionelle stood before her.

"Yes. I can tell Nandara how I got there. I did open a door to the demon realm, though I wasn't aware of what I was doing. I was digging for more and more power, focused only on destroying the water demons. The only way to get more power was to dig through the walls of reality and bring the realm of fire to us. I don't have the strength or the concentration to do that right now."

"Enough for now, then. Rest and we'll bring your findings to the Dragoness Superior," the dragoness said. "The council may be able to replicate your actions and combat the water demons without your direct involvement."

Neesha settled in next to Nandara, committed to taking rest for the duration of the trip. She'd gain far more energy in the last day, and there was plenty of time before they reached the city. Sharing the information so others could try to replicate what she had done was a wise move, but Neesha wanted to touch the fire realm again. To feel that raw power. To save the dragons herself.

If she didn't regain enough strength once they reached the dragon city, she knew she could draw on a demon for power. She'd laid waste to the water demons once already, and now she knew what she was doing. She would do it again.

CHAPTER FIFTEEN

T he dragons skimmed over red mountain peaks capped with snow despite the season. This was a landscape of contrasts, between the glistening white snow and glittering mica-speckled rock and the rich, verdant valleys blanketed with evergreens. Neesha couldn't enjoy the view. The red mountains meant they were close. Were they in time? There were patches of clouds on the horizon ahead of them, but that could mean anything. It could be natural mountain weather or the onset of a supernatural storm—or the end of one. There was nothing Neesha could do, so she simply watched the landscape disappear beneath them and tried not to fidget.

"There!" Dionelle called out, pointing straight ahead.

Neesha looked up, the clouds had parted just so and something towering above the clouds shimmered in the distance. The dragon city. That it was still standing was a joy after so much uncertainty.

Grinning, Neesha watched the city slowly come into focus. She'd forgotten how big it was, how it towered over the valley, jutting into the clouds. From afar it looked as though the city was floating. As they drew nearer, Neesha saw the obsidian and diamond support columns braced against the mountains. It was beautiful enough to make her forget, for just a moment, why she was there in the first place.

The dragoness brought them down into the valley, into the human settlement directly under the city while she went up to inform the council of their arrival. There were some stone buildings on the valley floor, though most of the structures were little more than tents made of sticks and tarps.

They were the last to arrive, and Nandara went to seek out the other wizards while Neesha rested, enjoying the astounding view.

The glimmering dragon city was all rounded and smoothed edges that spiralled up into the clouds, casting the afternoon sunlight into the valley and across the shimmering red mountains around them. Four support columns arched over the valley, two each of obsidian and diamond, each originating from the four points of the compass. They met above the centre of the valley, twisting around the bulbous base where the bulk of the city stood. From there, the imposing marvel reached skyward, graceful tendrils of obsidian and diamond entwining like a great flame. Smaller glittering towers of all different colours and gems dotted the mountainsides around the valley, casting multi-hued light in all directions. All of them were home to dragons.

Everything about the valley was peaceful and awe-inspiring. Neesha breathed deeply, enjoying the fresh scent of a place where winter was still far off.

Eventually, the dragoness came back to say that the council wanted to see her.

"They want to try to open the gate on their own. Draxli is not far off and we need to be quick."

Neesha hadn't noticed anything, but sat up and looked north, horrified by the sky growing dark with rain. Her pulse quickened as the dragoness picked her up and took to the sky, taking her into one of the large spires of diamond, skidding down the tunnel and gliding into the massive room below. The glittering chamber seemed endless, its arched buttresses obscuring its outer walls, the sheer number of dragons arranged in concentric circles and filling it seemed impossible. Neesha took a deep breath, ready to wield fire like not even a dragon could. She was tired but didn't doubt the abilities of the assembled wizards and dragons.

A snowy white dragoness stood in the centre of the crowd and the black dragoness left Neesha before her.

"We understand what you're capable of," the black dragoness explained. "We will provide you with fire to begin the process and will join in once you've summoned a demon. The more demons you can call to us, the more likely our success." She bowed and moved to her place in the middle of the crowd.

Neesha stood still, and focused her will where she knew it was needed. She was already beginning the spellcraft of the summoning when the entire chamber filled with a conflagration nearly matching the one she had created over Pasdale, though severely lacking the same bright intensity.

Demons sprang up into the light immediately, and Neesha had to focus on directing them to where they were needed without letting her guard down enough to be possessed. A dragon cried out, and then another, and soon a cacophony of dragons screeched into the flames, but she held the spell, calling more and more demons to her. The demons disappeared as quickly as she called them until most of the fire had vanished, leaving Neesha feeling slow and heavy. Only the oldest dragons remained.

Her black dragoness hastily approached, picking Neesha up.

"The attack has begun without time to open the way. The dragons have taken demon possession and have gone out to meet the battle. We are gathering some of the strongest dragons and the wizards at the edge of the valley," the dragoness said.

"I don't have the strength to open the way again."

"You do not have to. We need you to guide us. The dragons that remain will coax a portal from the demons you call. With that done, the other pyromancers will take up the battle and wield the energy from the fire realm."

"Will they be able to?" Neesha asked.

"They have been studying what you did, and the information Nandara brought them should be enough."

They exited the dragon city and Neesha stilled when she saw the rain coming down in a torrent, flooding the human settlement below.

"Where's Mamma? And Ondias?"

"They're with the other wizards. The other humans have been moved farther south."

Squinting through the rain, Neesha saw that the settlement, quickly being overrun by water, was empty. The sky was full of dragons and their fire.

The dragoness brought her to the southern point of the valley, farthest from the rain. The storm moved swiftly, pelting them the entire way to the southern edge, where the members of the Guild gathered with other dragons. A fire already blazed, and more and more demons came up out of it, taking possession of the dragons.

The dragoness set Neesha down near the fire, which was dwindling in the rain. Neesha immediately set to work and focused her will. Heat flared through her body, fire danced around her. It was like the battle for Pasdale. Her lips curved into a determined smile. Maybe she could open the way yet. With so many dragons on hand, the firestorm would be legendary. She heard the hiss and hoped for a moment that it was the language of the demon realm. But the fire's intensity faded from her eyes. The fire washed away in front of her.

"No!" she growled, doubling her efforts, feeling the same fear and determination as before, digging furiously for the strength to do more. The fire sputtered out. There was nothing left for her to work with.

"Mistress! I need fire!"

Dragons circled all around her, why weren't any of them giving her fire? They were supposed to be opening a portal.

Instead of fire, the dragoness snatched up her and Dionelle and headed farther south still. A silver dragon raised a jet of flame and Neesha seized on it, calling forth demons and trying to negotiate a fire portal. But before the dragoness could land to regroup, a wall of water cascaded over the shoulder of the northern mountain, washing around the support column. Ice dropped into her gut.

"No!"

With destructive force, the water dashed against the mountain, cracking it apart, all of it hanging suspended for one terrible instant. Then the rocks slid and tumbled, the rumble of it vibrating in her mind. The water churned red like blood with the stone of the mountainside entirely washed away, boulders and snapped trees crashing to the valley floor.

Dragons shrieked. Neesha pulled even more demons from the remnants of dragonflame. Their hissed language rang in her ears. Even as she struggled, she couldn't tear her gaze away from the carnage to the north. Her hand drifted over her mouth and she held her breath.

With its support washed away, the northern pillar of the city sank. The northern support collapsed. A crack like thunder split the world as the city ripped apart under the sheer weight of itself. The obsidian and diamond spires shattered and crumbled into the valley, which had become a churning lake, bloodlike with the dust of the Red Mountains.

Neesha held her breath, her head feeling light and her body far too heavy. Her rapid pulse hammered in her temples. She had to be dreaming. This had to be a nightmare born of worry. Surely she would wake up any moment to clear skies and glittering city.

This could not be possible.

Neesha, with so much power and surrounded by dragons, was supposed to save the city. Failure had never been an option. Pasdale had been a fluke. She knew what she was doing now. This wasn't right.

The dragons all fled, wailing as they streamed south like a flock of startled birds. Neesha's thoughts scattered with them, her breath caught in her throat as she stared forward at nothing. The dragoness stopped in the mountains south of the valley to deposit Dionelle and Neesha into the wagon where Ondias waited for them. Nandara was with another wizard travelling with their dragoness's cerulean mate and the pair of them took flight immediately, bringing their charges farther south.

From her place in the wagon, Neesha slowly turned north, but there was nothing but grey cloud and churning water to see. She couldn't look away.

The dragons fled well into the night, stopping only once they were out of the mountains and into the plains beyond. Neesha's human companions all bore the same grim silence and mantle of failure.

CHAPTER SIXTEEN

The silence eventually got to Neesha. The entire day-long trip south through the mountains to the desert had been silent. The silence became a presence all its own, heavy with grief and surreal amid the sheer numbers of humans and dragons gathered under stars that glittered like the shattered diamonds of the falling city. To be surrounded by so much life and yet so much silence was intolerable.

Neesha couldn't get the images of destruction out of her mind. She let go of her grief, curling on her blankets in the dust and wailing the loss beyond comprehension. How could she have so much power and be such a failure?

Dionelle silently placed a hand on her shoulder, a small comfort and a grand gesture. It was Ondias who joined Neesha in openly grieving, followed by a wizard Neesha didn't know, before Dionelle began sobbing so deeply that Neesha worried—in the background of her thoughts—that her mother may stop breathing altogether.

Once Dionelle broke down in her grief, the black dragoness embraced the emotion as well, sitting on her haunches and throwing her head back. The agonized howl she directed skyward echoed in the open air, her anguish reverberating off distant dunes. Others of her kin took up the chorus of grief. Two dragons had been overwhelmed by the water before they could retreat entirely and four humans had been lost in the deluge, including one of the pyromancers who had come to combat the threat.

Their pain lasted through the night, growing more acute as dawn rose on their bleak surroundings. The silence, at least, had been broken, replaced by shuffling sounds of moving bodies, whispered conversations without end, and punctuated by sobs and howls.

The noise was pitiful. Somehow the silence had been better. Loss turned to defeat.

Dionelle was the only dragon whisperer among them. The humans who had initially congregated at the edges of the grieving dragon mass approached her in the centre where Dionelle sat with her exhausted and despondent daughter.

Neesha was cold and numb, barely able to feel her body, emptied of fire, worthless in her failure.

"We need to return to the Guild," Fraxnir said. "We can aid the dragons as best we can during this most difficult time, but we cannot do so from these wastes."

Dionelle looked around blearily. The dragons lay in the dust in abject defeat, as if their very souls had died, and she drew in a slow, deep breath, rising up as she did. Neesha watched her approach the black dragoness, her dear friend, speaking softly so that no one else heard. The dragoness was nonresponsive for a time, but finally tilted her head to make direct eye contact with Dionelle.

At last the dragoness lifted her head, assessing their situation and seeming to notice all the humans in their midst for the first time. Dragon scholars and artisans from across the kingdoms who had been gathered to work with and study the creatures in their home had been caught up in the battle and were equally displaced.

"I don't want to go back to Pasdale," Ondias said, moving purposefully toward the dragoness.

Neesha was surprised to hear her voice ringing clear, the pain giving her strength and clarity.

"Mistress, I want to go back to the valley. It has been a home to me as much as it is to you. I don't want to go back to Pasdale. We must reclaim your home. We must rebuild."

The dragons nearby lifted their heads, watching Ondias as she stopped next to Dionelle, fixated on the dragoness they had first befriended and to whom they were closest. Neesha barely realized she had climbed to her feet until she saw herself being drawn closer to her mother and friends.

"Is that possible?" Neesha heard herself say, her voice sounding like it echoed down a long tunnel to reach her own ears. "Can it be rebuilt?"

"It was an ancient place," the dragoness said, "but the magic that created it has not been lost to us."

"We need to reclaim that land first," Ondias said. "We will rebuild your city and our settlement beneath it. But first we need to disperse the threats against it. The destruction of your city is only the beginning. There's no doubt in my mind that Draxli will continue to hunt your kind unless he is stopped."

"We need to be back at the Guild," Dionelle said. "We need to gather our strength there so that we can properly combat this threat. We were close—Neesha nearly had the way open. We need to replicate what she is capable of in a safe environment before we bring it into battle."

"Can it be replicated?" Neesha asked. "That's what we were supposed to do in the city and it didn't work."

"We didn't have the time to prepare. The attack came too swiftly and we were left reacting, scattered," Nandara said from behind Neesha.

"Yes, we need a concentrated effort," Dionelle said. "Draxli would be a true fool with utter lack of vision if he were to attack the Guild now. His intentions would become transparent. We will have time to combat him before he can spin the Guild into enemies."

"The Grand Chancellor has already spoken with his council present here and granted the dragons temporary refuge in the hills surrounding the Guild hall," Nandara said. "We can work together on the spellcraft required to counter Draxli's forces. Then we can offer you what aid we have in rebuilding."

The dragoness looked around at her kin, more of them gathering by the moment, and turned her attention back to Dionelle.

"As you know, I am not permitted to make decisions on behalf of the Superiors, but I will bring your proposal to them. I thank you for your offer of aid."

The dragoness stood then and made her way across the open plain to where the Dragoness Superior still mourned. Other dragons of the council and of the ruined city gathered as well, communicating in their native language while Dionelle brought Neesha and the other humans back to where the rest of their kind waited.

"I don't want to go to the Guild," Ondias said. "Neither do many of the others. We want to remain here, near the Red Mountains, and wait for victory so we can begin rebuilding immediately."

"If the dragons accept the offer of aid, they will bring us where we ask them to," Dionelle said. "Some of them will be more than willing to bring you to the foothills to wait. Many of them will not be ready to make the long journey to the Guild."

Neesha was weary with grief, her mind overrun by the image of the city crumbling into the swirling depths. The city she was supposed to save. The thought of travel was nearly unbearable—the weeklong journey to the Guild, stuck in isolation in that wagon—was more than she could cope with. If she couldn't go home, safe in her own bed, then she didn't want to go anywhere.

"I want to stay too," Neesha said.

Dionelle gave her a pitying look, draping an arm across her shoulders.

"We need you, Nee. You need to show them how to open the gates to the fire realm."

No one was surprised when the dragons accepted the offer for aid. One group of dragons took Ondias and the contingent of human settlers to the foothills to await the opportunity to rebuild. The rest began the trek to the Guild to prepare their attacks on Draxli's forces. With more dragons to bear the burden of ferrying the humans back to their realms, the journey went faster than Neesha expected, though she largely remained in a fog of grief.

Every night when they stopped, the wizards gathered, passing theories between each other, always trying to include Neesha, though she barely had the words to speak. Their ideas always came back to her opening the gate to let the power of the fire realm through. Finally, on the fourth night of their journey, she'd had enough.

She was huddled among the wizards in a ring around the fire, deep in the mountains about a day's flight from Pasdale. The dragons had taken their heat with them up into the snow-capped peaks, so Neesha was wrapped in blankets, toes edging toward the fire for warmth. She didn't look up as she spoke, her words laced with insight and despair.

"There's a better way to increase our fire power. Send me to the fire realm. Let my presence break down the barriers as it did when my mother spent so many months there. The dragons can do this easily, open a gate that goes to and not from."

"Absolutely not," Dionelle said. "There's no way to retrieve you."

"There's always a way. Pa came for you."

"And it took months for your mother's presence in that realm to cause the changes in demon influence that we would need to overthrow Draxli," Fraxnir argued. "There's no reason Draxli's forces couldn't seize on the opportunity your presence in the realm would present and use it as a means to ruin all of those who oppose him. He could use his demons to wash away all of Golden Hill and the kingdoms it encompasses."

"The changes began as soon as Dionelle entered the fire realm," Nandara said. "We were just unaware of them until the activity became so great. The demons themselves were unaware of the instability at first. The instability only grew out of control once the demons became more active. Dionelle leaving their realm stabilized everything."

"If I go there now, and only the fire demons are aware of the change, they can capitalize. If we are quick—if you, here in this realm, are quick enough in bringing fire to the water demons—you can end this before Draxli can respond. I could open far more than one gate for you if I am on the other side."

Dionelle touched Neesha's shoulder.

"I know that you are grieving, but you mustn't be rash about this decision. The demons will use trickery to entice you to stay."

"I know, I'll be ready. You were taken by surprise, but I have time to prepare. An entire city has been destroyed, an entire species has been left homeless and in despair. My one life seems a small thing in comparison."

Dionelle took her hand from her daughter's shoulder and rested it over the swell of her belly.

"You are more than just one life. And the only difference between my pregnancy with you and my mother's with me, is that I spent time in the fire realm. If that in itself was all that it would take to make you so much more powerful than I ever was, what will be the consequences this time, when you've already been doing so much to mix your essence with the demons?"

"Then it is two lives against the lives of all the dragons and who knows how many humans," Neesha said. "And even still, while the dangers are real this is hardly a death sentence for me. I don't have the strength left to open more gates from this side. Even once the baby comes, I will be too weak for far longer than we have time. Let me go. Let me weaken the boundaries."

"You wait until we reach the Guild," Fraxnir said. "We will begin our assault against Draxli the instant you are through to the fire realm."

"You cannot be considering this," Dionelle snapped at him.

"Your daughter is an adult and a member of the Guild, even if only temporarily," Fraxnir said. "The decision is hers, and it has more merit than anything else we have attempted thus far. Weakening the walls between the worlds gives us the opportunity to bring forth more demon strength than in just the location where we have your daughter present to aid us. We can defend the dragons' valley, the Guild, and the lands in between all at once. We can shut this down quickly and end it for good."

"Mamma, you have to let me try." Neesha kept her gaze fixed on the fire.

Dionelle stood abruptly and left the discussion, but Neesha would not be swayed by her mother's anger. She knew Dionelle had little power to influence the Guild's decision, especially with the dragons in such dire need. With the decision made, the message was sent to those dragons returning to their valley that they must leave fires burning at all points of battle so that portals could be opened from the other side.

Neesha was determined and focused, shaping her grief into something new, something that left her feeling less helpless. The remainder of the trip was solemn and quiet, as everyone processed their grief and Dionelle brooded. She hadn't spoken to Neesha since the decision had been made. A message for Lady Zyx was left in Pasdale with the wizards returning there, so she would know that aid was coming, though only Zev was trusted with the truth, instructed to watch for the instability.

By the time they reached Pasdale, they learned that Draxli's host was gathering strength, the forces from the attack on the dragon city rushing to join in on the siege. Neesha knew they needed to be quick and she worried over the two days to the Guild that they would be too late again.

She agonized over her family's fate, grateful that her mother was with her, even though she remained grudgingly silent.

Neesha's chest was so tight she could barely breathe when the dragons landed in the fields beyond the Guild's hillside entrance, where they rested while the returning wizards hurried inside to make plans with their remaining comrades. They had little news of what had been going on during the arduous journey from the ruined dragon city and needed to assess the situation before they could focus their attacks.

While Nandara and Dionelle went into the Guild, Neesha remained with the dragons. She left her supplies with the wagon and stood by the black dragoness.

"This is a brave and foolish thing you are about to do," the dragoness said.

"It must be done."

"We are indebted to you for all you have done to aid us."

"I've done nothing," Neesha growled, staring out over the hillside. "I won't fail this time."

Neesha was grateful that the dragoness respected her enough not to bombard her with platitudes. While Neesha accepted that there simply hadn't been the time for the Guild's forces to organize themselves and save the city, she still felt guilty. She had the power to stop Draxli. That she hadn't yet was unforgiveable.

"We can begin as soon as your mother returns," the dragoness said.

"Is that all we're waiting for? Send for her then, and let's begin. We've waited too long already and I fear Pasdale's fate."

While the dragoness took flight, heading to the dragon entrance on the hilltop, Neesha stripped down to her skin, removing anything that would burn, and then wrapped herself in the amethyst firecloak. She waited quietly on the edge of the circle formed by the Superiors until the Dragoness Superior heeded Neesha's presence.

"I'm ready," Neesha said. "We shouldn't wait."

The dragoness sent the instructions to the gathered dragons in that language Neesha barely recognized as a language at all, and the black dragoness appeared out of the air, bearing Dionelle with her. Dionelle remained silent but desperately clung to Neesha, almost as if she were trying to hold her daughter within the reality she knew.

"It's time, Mamma."

"Be quick. Don't linger."

Dionelle backed away and stood near the edge of the circle of Superiors. The dragons lifted their heads to the sky, dozens of living torches blazing toward the heavens, and then as one, when their firecraft had reached its climax, they leaned forward and bathed Neesha in flame.

She kept her eyes open against the light, no matter how much it made her mind ache and her eyes water. She knew the instant she was in the fire realm, as the fire took on a discernable shape. The realm's heat chased away the chill that had settled in her heart after the dragon city fell. Warm peace settled over her.

It was hard to believe she was here. Hard to will herself to take that first step, certain she would sink down into a ground made of fire. She had always listened raptly when her parents had spoken of their time in this realm, but she was still astounded to see it, a world of living light. Even the sky burned. It reminded her of that first battle in Pasdale.

"Now what...?"

There was no sign of the way she had come, no gate behind her that she could simply push open to send the power of the fire realm back through.

Dionelle had refused to discuss the plan at all, and it had been Nandara who had done her best to guide Neesha on making a portal from the fire realm to the world in which she belonged. So she thought of Ondias, hoped the woman guarded a fire in the Red Mountains, and opened a gate, but not so that she could go through. She merely had to think *gate* and send a puff of energy out. The power tingled through her. As easy as pulling fire out of fire, as natural as any other spellcraft she had ever cast.

Beside the first gate, she opened a second one to the Guild, focusing on her mother and the dragoness, knowing they would have a flame nearby. Then she thought of her family in Pasdale, but knew better than to send a portal to their hearth. She shifted her focus to Lady Zyx, holding their one encounter in her mind, mixing Zev into her thoughts and pulling open a final portal.

This had to work. It *had* to. Draxli had strong aquamancers, to be sure, but none of them had elemental essence the way Neesha did. She tried to envision him being vaporized by the pure flame from the realm. Did any of it work like that? Would demons go through on their own? Had they already?

Neesha glanced around, wondering what the demons looked like in this realm. She hoped the other pyromancers back in Pasdale were getting what they needed from those portals. There was no way for Neesha to tell if it was working.

Now that she was actually here, surrounded by such beauty with such a capacity for destruction, the risks inherent in the plan were more obvious. Of course, the risk of doing nothing was far greater. She faced doom one way or another.

She'd be damned if she didn't go down fighting.

CHAPTER SEVENTEEN

Three swirling amber lights hovered in front of Neesha as she sat on the warm, comforting ground. Used to her surroundings, no longer concerned she would sink forever into the fire. She was surprised by how calm and energized she felt, the baby turning somersaults in her belly, bouncing around like it hadn't since before the battle for Pasdale. She was alert and awake too, and cast around, wondering where all the demons were. If they hadn't gone through her portals yet, she needed to find them and help them along.

"Can I do a summoning here? Or should I just stand around and let them find me?"

She hadn't thought to discuss how long she should stay in the realm, how long they would need. Did she need to stay? There was no way of knowing if the portals would all stay open if she left. She knew she could stay there for months before it made the walls so thin that it endangered her loved ones. Of course, now that the demons knew what to look for, they might become active much sooner.

"You know what, let's just stay here," Neesha said to her belly. "You can decide when we go back."

She hadn't spoken with the midwife enough to know fully what to expect yet, that conversation had been slated for a few days after she'd last been in Pasdale. But it would be unmistakable when the baby was imminent. So that, at the very least, would be her signal to go home.

In the meantime, she studied the world around her more closely, now that she'd done what she'd initially set out to do. The ground beneath her was burning embers. They were rough but hadn't crumbled when she walked on them the way they did when she walked through fires at home. The ground was a dark reddish orange and the sky blazed bright. Swirling pillars of fire rose up, flaring out above her like flaming trees. She wanted to explore, but wasn't sure if she should leave the portals. Anything could go wrong with them sitting open.

She caught sight of movement in the distance, an increased intensity to the flickering lights of the horizon and watched as it drew closer, slowly able to discern the bright, crawling shape of a demon coming her way. As she waited, more and more appeared around her, closing in. They spoke but she wasn't entirely sure if they were talking to each other or to her.

Before long, she was entirely surrounded. Their voices made strange sense to her, though the words weren't coming out in a language she understood. There were inquires, thoughts suddenly appearing in her mind, and she focused on thoughts to send back to them, trying to show them what was going on in the world beyond. To show them what they needed to do.

There was a pause filled with strange silence, the demons regarding each other.

Can they communicate without words?

In an instant they were in motion, funnelling through the three portals while Neesha watched on in shock.

"Wait! Where are you going? What are you doing! Don't hurt my family!"

She wasn't sure if they were intent on aid or mischief, or if they would be a hindrance to what was going on in the world beyond. She felt a strong sense of purpose to their movements, and she hoped there were pyromancers in place on the other side of her portals, ready to direct the demons. Neesha lost all sense of time as hundreds of demons slipped between worlds like leaves being sucked down rapids. Roughly a dozen remained.

"Have they gone to stop the water?" she asked. "They need to leave the people alone. Do they understand that? Just the water. Let the people deal with the people."

She got an immediate image in her mind of water boiling and sizzling against heat, like lava meeting the ocean. Liquid fire moved toward the water, a great onslaught of fire that would not be put out. She tried parsing out what they meant. Clearly, they were sending her a message, though she couldn't precisely understand these visions.

Neesha curled on the ground, watching the demons who had simply gathered around her, like barn cats observing her milk the cows. They had treated her mother like a novelty as well. She had to guard herself against any trickery, against any messages urging her to remain in their midst. The baby would signal it was time to head back before things got as out of hand as they had with Dionelle.

Neesha had a week at most.

Despite her misgivings, she was curious about how she felt energized and satiated, well rested despite the long, trying journey. And nothing ached. She couldn't remember the last time her body hadn't caused her grief. There was no one to judge her or shame her or coerce her into bad situations. She sank into the heat and embraced it, letting it burn away the misery of the last several months. She wasn't hungry or thirsty or cold or tired. The energy of the realm surrounded her, and she knew enough about her essence to know that it could sustain her—that the part of her that was fire demon took the energy around her and converted it into her life force.

Neesha concentrated on that energy, trying to be conscious of it, wanting to manipulate it. She knew her mother had been able to perform spells in this realm, and Neesha wanted to do more than open portals for the demons. The energy she had accidentally pulled from this realm during that first battle had been what really made the difference against the water demons. None of the other pyromancers could do what she had.

So she focused on her surroundings, feeling the burning life all around her. It was full of emotion—passion, fury, and fear—that she quickly tuned into and shaped with her will. She funnelled it through each of the three portals, wondering if any of the pyromancers could wield it or if that feat would rest on the demons she had let out into the world.

She didn't send them much, knowing they wouldn't need it unless things had gone poorly. She tried not to think of Draxli figuring out what they had done, though she didn't think there was any reason why he should have known any of the details of her mother's whereabouts while she was missing. That information was supposed to be guarded by the Guild, who had been solely in charge of the investigation since the Dunhams had written her off as dead.

Neesha could only wait, with her entourage of demons for company. They tried to wear her down with their thoughts, inviting her to stay. To close the portals and curl up in their midst forever. It seemed like a good idea, but she held in her mind what would happen to the world if she did. She and her mother would survive the collapse for a little while, but even then their human essences would eventually be destroyed.

She lay back, staring up at the intense sky that should have been a strain on her vision, basking in how good she felt after feeling awful for so long. Even the burden of her child was lighter than it ever had been. There was no judgement here, no responsibility. Just warmth and comfort.

"No wonder Pa couldn't get Mamma to leave," she said to the baby. "I've got you, at least."

She couldn't have the child in the fire realm.

Why not?

It couldn't be safe. Or could it? The baby would be as much fire demon as Neesha. They'd both be sustained here. Her mother could come for her if they really needed her.

Do they ever need you?

Neesha sat up, shocked by the clarity of that thought and by the knowledge that it had not come from her. It had been a simple question, but loaded as well. She knew it was trickery, but it was far more enticing than she ever imagined.

Why couldn't she remain in the fire realm with her child? The energies there would support her through the birth the same as any midwife or healer. If complications arose, she would die or she wouldn't, regardless of which realm she was in. Her mother had come back because she'd been worried that Neesha wouldn't have survived birth in the realm, but they hadn't understood then that the demon essence could be passed mother to child. Neesha's baby would have demon essence at least as strong as her own and would undoubtedly survive in the realm just as well as she was now.

"Tempting." She looked around at the demons, wondering which of them had sent the message, or if it was a concentrated effort.

Neesha resolved to stay until the baby came and settled in, soaking in the energy and letting it envelope her in the heat. She moved to a nearby spout of fire and was delighted to discover that she could rest on top of it. It was far softer than anything she felt before, like resting on a cloud, but so comfortably warm and cozy that she was disinclined to get up. She had a clear view of the portals, so it was an ideal place to rest. The remaining demons gathered under the firespout she'd taken command of.

She closed her eyes, meaning only to focus on the comfort after so many weeks of misery and pain, but must have fallen asleep. It was Dionelle's voice that woke her.

"Neesha!"

She felt the pressure of a hand squeezing her arm. Her mother stood before her. Surrounded by so much light, Neesha hadn't had a sense of distance or size, and the spout was only a little taller than her bed at home. She rested at the same height as her mother's waist.

Dionelle bent over her, her face drawn out with concern.

"Nee, you need to come with me. Now. We need you."

"No, Mamma. It's too beautiful here. It's so peaceful."

"Baby, you know what happens if you stay." She took a sharp breath. "You said you wouldn't let them sway you."

"They're not swaying me. I haven't felt this light and at peace since I was a little girl."

"Neesha, I know things haven't been easy. But you need to come home now. You've unleashed demons on the world. You have to close your gates. Please, come back. You have to help us control them."

Neesha was prepared to argue when she noticed the grimace fixed on her mother's face.

"Mamma! You left your immunity behind the last time you were here. How are you even here?"

"The flame won't harm me."

"But it hurts you! You can feel it. Mamma, you have to go back!"

"I'm not leaving without you." Dionelle shook her head emphatically. "The pain will numb. I just have to remember that the pain is a false sensation."

"I'll come home soon, but you need to go. You'll drive yourself mad in this, even the ground is fire!"

Dionelle had done as Neesha had and had stripped, wearing only the firecloak, so she was barefoot on the embers.

"Go back! I will come soon. I just want to stay until the baby is ready."

"You think you came to that conclusion on your own, but I promise you it's the demons. Their trickery is subtle." Dionelle squeezed her eyes shut and took an uneasy breath. "It gradually builds on itself until they have taken all of your thoughts. Come now, or when the pain of the baby's arrival starts, you will convince yourself the realm will protect you. That it will provide for you more than the midwife ever could."

Neesha didn't like that she'd had that very thought. Her concern was for her mother. She had never been able to experience the full pain of burning—it had always been a sensation that remained in the periphery of her senses and not something that actually affected her. She did know pain, though, and she knew that her mother was in terrible pain just by being there. The very air around them was alive with heat.

"Mamma..." Neesha paused when she felt something tug at her stomach. She'd noticed it a few times, but this pull suddenly became a tear, like her body was trying to rip itself in half, and it stopped her in the middle of her thought, doubling her over.

"Nee, darling, what is it?"

"Hurts," she whispered through gritted teeth, shuffling off her fiery perch to crouch next to her mother.

"Where?"

Neesha pressed her hands over her belly, right over the middle, right at the top of her pelvis. The pain finally receded. She grunted her relief and stood.

"The baby," Dionelle said. "It's time to go."

Neesha wanted to argue, but knew her mother was right about the pain. The fact that she wanted to stay meant Dionelle was right about the demons as well.

Her baby was coming. Now.

Not even the fire realm could push back the chill she felt. Time to go.

It was the dragon chamber and not the healer's ward that Neesha stood in, waiting for aid, often doubling over into a crouch as birth pains tore through her body. When they passed through the fire portal and into a large hearth at the centre of the Wizard's Guild compound, it wasn't the healer Neesha had asked for first. It was the dragoness.

Neesha was alone for the moment. It wouldn't be long before her mother or the dragoness or the healer joined her. But she was cold. And trembling.

She'd spent so much time preparing for battle that she'd forgotten about this part. Now she was vastly unprepared.

Before the fear had the chance to paralyze her, the black dragoness slid in through the opening near the ceiling and glided down to her. Watching the great beast drew her attention to the vast chamber. Unlike the drab grey stone of the other rooms she'd seen in the Guild, this one had been painted with a stunning mural of the night sky. Silvery paint had been flecked on to give a shimmery quality to the stars.

The presence of the dragoness was comforting, much like the warmth of the fire realm had been. The beast was silent, but lay on the floor near Neesha, the heat of her filling the room.

Dionelle returned not long afterward, her expression grim. Her hair was unkempt and her clothing askew.

"Mamma, how long was I gone?"

"It is late the same day you left," Dionelle said. "We need your help, Neesha. The power you sent through is good, it's helping, but some of the demons are intent on mischief and only making things worse for everyone. We're beating back the water demons and Draxli's forces, but the fire demons are causing as much damage as they're helping. We need to close off the portals and send them back. They've overrun the city."

Neesha leaned her head back with her hands braced against her lower back and squeezed her eyes shut in frustration. She knew they were in for a long night, that the baby would need its time to arrive safely. She followed the warmth radiating from the dragoness, tried to follow it to the portals she'd opened. There was no way to touch them from where she was. And then another painful tremor rent her body.

She could be of no use. Not right now.

"I'm scared," she said.

Dionelle drew closer and cupped Neesha's cheek with her hand. "I know, my darling, but it will be all right."

"Please don't lie to me."

"It will," Dionelle said, a hint of amber flashing in her expression. Neesha rarely saw it in her mother's blue eyes.

"You're going to help me?"

"My dear girl, you are going to need so much help. So much more than you realize. After all that you have done—you have grown up so much in this last month—you have made up for the hardships you've caused. You've far exceeded it."

"I'm sorry about this. I didn't mean for it."

"Don't apologize for the baby. We will love your child just as we love you."

Dionelle squeezed her hand and helped her to sit next to the dragoness.

"How can I assist you?" the dragoness asked.

Neesha only whimpered as the pain tore through her centre of being. Dionelle addressed the dragoness.

"Mistress, we'll need to keep her as comfortable as we can. She's been re-energized by the fire realm, and it will help to keep her strong through this, but she will need to brace herself in a few hours' time."

Neesha remembered what the midwife had told her and was unsurprised when the healer arrived with a basket padded by blankets, one of them nothing more than a thick bandage covering the rest. She would crouch over this when the time came, and she would be helped to balance while someone else guided the baby into it. Until then, she could sit. She was surprised when the dragoness drew her near, enveloping her with her massive foreleg. Neesha rest in the crook of her elbow.

Neesha lost herself to the pain and the fear, gone strangely numb, trying her best to focus on her mother's instructions and the healer's reports. The healer was an old woman—likely older still than even Fraxnir—and she trusted the woman had been around for the birth of many babies. Neesha was still in her firecloak, and whenever the healer tried to wash something away, the dragoness would cleanse the area with fire. It helped bring a small measure of comfort, the heat of dragonflame eased her pain, and the stunning expanse of the night sky mural brought Neesha back to the tranquility of the mountain passes. She focused on how the stars glittered to distract from the worst of the pain.

The time came to stand and Nandara had joined them by then. The dragoness let Neesha brace herself against one massive hand while Nandara and Dionelle steadied her on either side. She had already screamed herself hoarse, wishing she had stayed in the fire realm through this. Everything ached. She was exhausted but alert. The relief of the baby coming into the world was instant and intense. She felt lighter. The burning agony subsided. Even before the women gasped and the baby began crying, Neesha knew it was over.

Neesha turned and collapsed against the dragoness. The hollow place inside of her rapidly filled with relief.

"Let me see."

"A girl," Dionelle said, cradling the baby in a fresh blanket and clearing away some of the mess.

The baby was dazzling white, like a winter night under the moons. She blinked her eyes open between whimpers and all three women gasped to see that her eyes were fully amber, all flame and no natural colour at all.

Neesha had never seen anything so beautiful. Her thoughts were still and she felt pleasantly lightheaded.

"She is fireborn," the dragoness said. "Set her on the stone and let me help you clean her."

Neesha felt a swell of pride when the dragoness bathed the baby in fire, burning away the last traces of her entry to the world while the healer tended to the last of Neesha's needs. Neesha felt hollowed out, not only because her womb was empty after so many months, but because the ordeal was over and something completely new would begin.

Now she held her baby girl.

"Do you have a name for her?" Dionelle asked gently.

The question seemed so strange after her entire family had done their best to avoid even acknowledging the baby's very being. She hadn't discussed any of her intentions or hopes, not even what possible names she might give her child.

"Mita," she said.

"The dragons' patron goddess of flame." Dionelle smiled.

"I think I knew she would be a girl," Neesha said. "I never did consider what to name a boy."

"It's the right name for her," Dionelle said.

Neesha cradled her daughter against her, pulling open the front of her robes to hold the baby against her skin, feeling the heat of the babe there, her life's force even warmer than Dionelle's. Neesha wondered what gifts the girl would have as she grew and how she may help the world in ways that even Neesha couldn't imagine.

She took some time to hold the baby and to take in her appearance, watching her in wonder as she clumsily let the girl suckle. Neesha's heart hurt in the most joyous way. Tired as she was, buzzing anger left Neesha's thoughts clear. Fury she had never known before rose up out her fiery depths. She knew what she needed to do.

"Draxli would never let her live." Neesha clenched her jaw. "We need to end him now."

CHAPTER EIGHTEEN

Reiser stood facing west, not caring one lick that he couldn't see the mountains through the heavy rain and thick clouds. Dionelle going to the dragon city had never bothered him before, but this time was different. If they weren't coming home, he might never know. He couldn't bear that kind of uncertainty again. He tried to lessen his resentment for Neesha, but Dionelle had only gone to help the girl, and if something happened to his wife as a result, he knew he wouldn't be able to help hating his daughter to the end of his days.

He hadn't been to the dragon city since he'd travelled there out of necessity. That many dragons was far too overwhelming, and Dionelle's trips out there had often taken up entire moon cycles. It was too long for him to be away from home and so far out of his element. He would have liked to have gone this time, despite the element of danger, maybe even because of it. So he kept vigil for their return, trying not to resent that he hadn't been considered and had barely been consulted.

Why couldn't he keep her safe?

There was still no sign of them, and in this downpour he wouldn't know they were coming until the dragoness set them down in the field. He was about to head inside when he spotted the dark smudge on the road to the south that could only be Bly returning from the market. The boy made slow progress on the boggy road, leading the horse rather than burdening it with his weight in addition to the supplies he had fetched. But he had been sent into the city as much to gather supplies as information.

"Water demons again," Bly said, confirming their suspicions. "The river started rising on its own before the rains moved in. The flooding will be worse than last time."

He brought the horse right up to the porch, and Reiser helped him unload the supplies for the homestead.

"Will Ma and Nee be home soon?"

Reiser shook his head. His stomach clenched. If Draxli was renewing his efforts against Pasdale, it was likely things had gone in his favour at the dragon city. What that meant for Dionelle and Neesha, he could only guess.

"If they didn't linger in the city, they should have been back by now," Reiser said. "I will have to make some inquiries with Zev, and see if he has heard anything from Nandara."

"You shouldn't wait, then," Bly said gravely. "You'll be lucky to make it into the city at all, even if you leave now. You'll be even less likely to make it back home again without a raft."

Reiser sighed and picked up the pace, unloading supplies so Bly could get the animal stabled. He called in to Breen to come help carry the supplies into the house and put them away.

"I'm going to the city to find news of your mother," he said. "Let Nanny know and help her out as much as you can. Get her over here, the flooding is worse than last time and could take you by surprise."

The old farmhouse had fared well through the last flood, but it wasn't nearly as sturdy as the stone house, which also had the added advantage of being on slightly higher ground.

Reiser left while the boy was dealing with supplies and before Sharice arrived and tried to coax him to stay.

He had gone far enough that turning back would have been as dangerous as continuing onward when a vortex of fire whirled up from the centre of the city. It lit up the gloomy twilight like some vengeful sunrise. He stood frozen in place as it lashed at the clouds, pulsing up from the palace, the roar of it barely audible over the falling rain and the sizzle of water being boiled into steam. By the time Reiser convinced his legs to move, the light had evanesced and the city had been consumed by thick fog that glowed as if on fire.

He trudged miserably through the muck, which was ankle deep with water up to his knees in some places. The rain had eased but the water had not receded and the thick fog continued to hamper his progress. What should have been a quick trip was an hours-long ordeal that left a leaden ache in his legs by the time he reached the city. The water was just as deep here, but at least the cobblestones offered better footing than the mud.

The city glowed like it was on fire, but Reiser couldn't smell any smoke through the rain. The fog was thick, obscuring anything that the rain didn't. He sloshed over the streets, first making his way toward the market, wondering if anyone would be there. The closer he got to the centre of the city, the brighter his surroundings. There were flashes of bright light at the edge of his vision and shouting came from the direction of the palace.

When he reached the market, the few merchants left hurried to pack up, even though there were hours left before traditional closing. Stone was there and the first one to notice and call him over.

"Did you just reach the city?" Stone asked. "How are the roads?"

"You'll never get a wagon through," Reiser said gravely. "Bly got through with the horse earlier this afternoon, but it's deteriorated since then. I don't plan to stay in the city long. What are these strange lights?"

Stone looked startled by the question. "I would have thought you'd know. It's not Neesha or your wife?"

"It could be. I hope it is. I've had no news of them since they left for the dragon city."

"I've heard rumours of fire demons," Stone said. "That requires high-level pyromancy."

Reiser nodded, feeling some hope. Lots of elementals could call on fire demons, but it could mean Dionelle was here and safe.

"Have there been any water demons yet? Is that why there are fire demons?"

Stone spread his hands in a gesture of helplessness. "We've heard little about what's going on. Since the initial flare, I've just been trying to get everything packed up to go home." He took a deep breath. "If the roads are impassable, then I just want to get to shelter. I feel a battle brewing."

Reiser clenched his jaw and gave a terse nod. Things were certainly not going well. He bid Stone farewell and made his way deeper into the city, heading for the palace to see if he could find Zev and hopefully some answers. As he trudged down one of the wide avenues, trying to stay near the buildings to maintain his balance in the poor conditions, he saw more of the flashing lights in the gloom.

Then a familiar hiss came toward him, and he tucked himself into a recessed doorway as a bright light approached. He knew it was a fire demon before it sizzled past him, leaving a trail of boiling water in its wake. Across the street, a blaze of them rushed by. It was hard to tell through the fog, but it looked like there was close to a dozen of them. He contemplated turning back, but with so many of them on the loose, it was possible Dionelle was nearby. He needed to know that she was safe. He had to keep going.

As he neared the palace, the water barely sloshed over the toe of his boot. The palace itself was on an artificial hill so that it rose above the rest of the city, but all the areas around it were level with each other. Although the rain had waned to a drizzle, the fog was still thick. He saw little more than a few feet in front of him. The city may have been crawling with fire demons, but at least they were making a difference. He might have a chance of making it back home.

He pressed onward, but it was much noisier toward the palace and he didn't like it. There were shouts and far more sizzling water. The water vapour in the air made it difficult to breathe. Metal clanged against metal. Some kind of battle. He had never heard real war before and didn't know what to make of it. He paused, uncertain if it was safe to continue when panicked shouting drew near and several figures materialized out of the gloom. Reiser pressed himself against the building to get out of their way.

There were three men, one wearing the bright armour of the palace guard. They were crying out, all shouting something different in the same frantic tones, and it wasn't until they had just about reached him that he was able to make out what they said.

The palace grounds were overrun with fire demons and nearly completely deluged with water, even if it was receding in the rest of the city. But worst of all, Lady Zyx had been killed. Reiser froze at the horror of that—at the city being left leaderless at such a time. Going to the palace would be a bad idea. But he didn't know where else to find Zev or information about his family. He sensed the impending instability at the news of Zyx's demise. The best place for him was home.

He was no warrior, and this had become a battleground for wizards. He would do his family no good getting killed on a fool's errand. And with the attack coming from the north, their home may yet see battle.

He didn't linger and rushed after the fleeing men, not stopping at the market this time. The rain was persistent outside the city, but at least the water was no longer rising. The wind had shifted and the fog cleared out so that he didn't have to make the trek in the fog and the darkness. It still took nearly twice as long as it should have for him to get home.

As he drew nearer, he spotted Sharice's worried face at the window watching for him. She didn't see him in the darkness until he reached the bottom of the porch steps, but her entire countenance sagged in relief. She met him at the door.

He relayed what he'd discovered while she helped him out of his muddy boots and cloak. The boys waited for him near the hearth in the parlour, but they'd heard him speaking to Sharice and there was little more to say.

"You boys should get to sleep. We'll need to be prepared for what tomorrow brings."

Reiser sent Sharice to bed as well, not wanting to have company while he fretted about Dionelle's fate. He threw a couple of extra logs on the fire, but not because he needed the warmth. It felt right. Had she made another trip to the demon realm? Shuddering, he settled in on the sofa, not expecting to sleep as his thoughts swirled around what the morning would bring.

Reiser only realized he'd fallen asleep at all when he was awakened by a knock at the door. As he stumbled sleepily toward the door, gentle light in the east told him that dawn wasn't far off. It was brighter than it had been the day before, but there were still rainclouds dotting the sky.

Zev stood on the doorstep. Reiser felt a burden lift, the knots in his chest unravelling even as his brow furrowed, desperate to hear what tidings the man brought.

"Good news or bad," Reiser said immediately, not bothering with formalities.

"Some of both." He started to tell Reiser about Lady Zyx, but Reiser cut him off, explaining what he already knew. "The demons were let into the city by Neesha—she went to the fire realm to unbalance the elements in our favour, but we weren't able to channel the power of that realm like she can. It allowed uncountable numbers of demons to come into our world and mount a defense against the water, but we haven't got enough wizards to control the demons and keep them focused."

"So they've been causing mayhem," Reiser said.

"Yes, I'm afraid so. They've done more to help, but Draxli's whispers already have people doubting the truth of it. His people have infiltrated our ranks and poisoned a lot of minds. Without Lady Zyx to combat the rumours, I don't know if we can undo the damage."

"And what of Dionelle?"

"She's at the Guild working with Nandara to guide your daughter as best anyone can."

Warm relief washed over him, his body uncoiling from the pent-up tension of not knowing. No matter what else Zev had to say, Reiser took comfort in knowledge of his wife's safety.

"When can I expect her back from the Guild?"

"That's the real reason I wanted to come here personally." Zev took a breath. "You have a granddaughter, Nandara has told me. The little one's name is Mita. Neesha is more determined than ever to wield her power against Draxli, but I'm uncertain of her condition, given what's happened."

A granddaughter. His breath caught in his chest and a smile touched his lips. While he found it difficult to muster goodwill toward his daughter, the news still warmed him. It was a little harder to keep hating her. And clearly some of her spellcraft made a difference in the night.

But the battle was clearly a long way from over.

"What should we do, about the demons?" he asked. "Should we try to leave?"

Zev shook his head. "Stay here. And you'll probably want to stay indoors. The waters are rising again, and our pyromancers are having difficulties keeping on top of the battle. Draxli's forces have boats and rafts and they are hours away from the city. You're safer away from Pasdale, but

I don't believe there is any escape from this valley, unless it's by the wings of a dragon."

Reiser nodded, not reassured by this last bit of news. Zev left and Reiser was unsurprised that the man had made it out to them via raft. Two aides waited for him on it and they ferried him back toward the city while Reiser delivered the news to his family. They weren't quite done being idle, biding their time.

There was some good news in it, at least. He looked forward to welcoming his granddaughter home once it was all over.

CHAPTER NINETEEN

Draxli held firm the reins on his serpent as he rounded the final hill. Home. At last. The valley of Pasdale spread out before him, a vast abyss swallowed by dark waters, thick clouds illuminated only by moonlight blocking all other light from reaching the valley. Tiny dots of lantern light speckled the floodplain ahead of him where his scouts waited for the bulk of his host to arrive. There was an entire armada at his back. He didn't care how flimsy the small, hastily crafted vessels were. Some were little more than rafts.

The water did all the work for them, guided by Loch and the other aquamancers. With a little more effort from the aquamancers, Draxli was certain the boats would have been unnecessary and they could have stood on the waves without a care.

As his water beast reached the lead rafts, a vicious flare of trueflame spewed out from the palace, momentarily lighting the city and punching a vast hole in the storm clouds, causing them to thin and shrink away before his eyes.

He ground his teeth and shouted back down the ranks for Loch. The boy couldn't be too far behind, but Draxli was ready to box his ears for not maintaining a closer distance. Draxli had instructed the boy to stay close, intending for them to arrive together.

"Report," Draxli snapped to his lead scout.

"We haven't heard back in an hour, sir, but everything was going according to plan at last check. There's been increased firelight since just after the last report."

"The waters should be higher. That city should be nearly gone by now."

"There's been resistance, sir."

"Zyx is still alive then. Your primary directive was to finish that meddling woman."

"M'lord, we have done all that we can."

Draxli felt as though he could strangle the words right out of the man's mouth, that he could reach through this insolent fool's death and take Zyx down on his own. He resisted the urge and turned to look at the city. His voice was calm, with only a hint of irritation.

"I know of only two pyromancers with the strength for something like this. They must be found. They must be killed. We cannot retake this land while they still breathe. Do you hear me?"

"Of course, m'lord. The young one is easy enough to spot. Her mother is never far behind."

Draxli nodded and watched out into the night. He had learned over the years that Dionelle had lost much of the oddity about her, though not her power. Her whelp, however, was every bit as white as the woman herself had been the last time Draxli had had the misfortune of laying eyes upon her. Draxli remembered the way to her farm, not far—just to the west of his position. He looked forward to taking her fool of a husband apart, skinning him alive before feeding the man to his water beast.

Draxli smiled at the thought.

He was tempted to go there now, but the farm and its inhabitants weren't going anywhere in this deluge. If they hadn't already drowned. Best to stay focused. Dionelle had been bad enough to deal with, but it was her husband who had been Draxli's real undoing. If the man had shut his mouth and let Karth replace the whisperer, there would have been no need for any of this. Karth would be alive, they'd have a whisperer they could actually work with, and Draxli would hold the seat of power that was rightfully his. Dionelle would have turned up eventually, as she had in the end, and that made little difference to him.

He tried to push away thoughts of the past, but it was difficult to see the valley he had once loved so much inundated and destroyed because of a pair of meddlers. A whole family of meddlers. Draxli had even heard rumours that the whelp was about to have a litter of her own. He couldn't stand the thought of it. He'd drown the entire city and build it up from scratch if that was what it took to wipe the Joaseras and their blasted dragons from the world.

"Have there been any dragon sightings?" Draxli asked.

Many of the dragons had tried to head him off at the dragon city, and it burned him that so many had escaped the deluge there. He did not want a repeat, did not want the beasts to escape. Failure to bring down the bulk of the dragons quickly this time would greatly complicate his plans.

"No, m'lord. Scouts to the west say there is a great force of them to the south of the Red Mountains, almost a day's ride from the river—far out in the desert."

"Very wise of them," Draxli growled. He had hoped to see them trying to guard the valley.

"Heard a report that some of them flew east, a small contingent, perhaps a dozen. They didn't come here."

This troubled Draxli. They were either lying in wait in the Great Mountains, biding their time, or they'd gone all the way to the Wizards Guild. He wondered if he had the power to face the whole of the Guild.

He turned his thoughts back to the present when Loch joined him.

"The city is beautiful, m'lord! I can see why you'd pine for it."

The boy's eyes shone in the moonlight, utterly rapt, and Draxli had to remind himself that the boy was a bumpkin who hadn't left his farming village until his failed attempt at joining the Guild. Many of the men at his back had never seen even the shoddy farm shacks the boy was used to until Draxli had come to them and started turning things around.

"It will be mine again soon enough. But those meddling pyromancers are providing more resistance than I'd like. We need your skill to get the waters rising. Another wave may be in order."

Loch shook himself from his reverie and looked at Draxli.

"M'lord, that is a huge city. All those people..."

"They're complicit," he said dismissively. "Zyx will be gone soon, and most of them will come to us for mercy. The rest..." He shrugged.

The boy swallowed hard and turned back to the city.

"This city is the root of our problems," Draxli crooned. "Without it, without those pyromancers, there won't be anyone left to indulge the dragons. They will lose their staunchest allies, and those who don't return to the wild where they belong to be ruled by our good friends..." He gestured to the four dragons hovering in the skies behind them. "Those will fall beneath your mighty waters. Prosperity will belong to the people again."

The boy's eyes glittered as he considered the possibilities, but Draxli saw his continued reservations in the way he furrowed his brow.

"Without having to divert so many resources to appeasing the beasts, just think of the harvests we'll see again. Your waters will aid them, and they'll sing songs of your victory. I'll commission the first myself."

The boy grinned, and Draxli smiled wolfishly, satisfied that he had the boy right where he needed him to be.

A wave rolled out from beneath them, causing the scouts' puny lantern lights to bob in the distance as their rafts rocked gently. The wave sped on, curling toward the city and further raising the water level.

It was a short wait before a new raft came in from the city, moving unnaturally fast on sympathetic waters, and Draxli sensed the jubilance of the two men on board.

"We've done it, m'lord!" one of them called out upon realizing that Draxli was present. "We drew her out enough for the waters to take her. Demons tried to stop us, but only boiled the waters around her so she never had a chance."

"Zyx is dead, then? You're certain?" He barely contained his glee.

"Yes, m'lord." The man bowed as his raft pulled alongside Draxli on his serpent. "Saw it with me own eyes. Saw her go under, saw the water boil around her. One o' her own, screaming for healers like a fool, finally pulled her out. Even in the torchlight I could see she was gone."

A sly grin spread across Draxli's face.

"We have them now!"

He called for specific aquamancers. Once they were gathered before him, he drew up his serpent, its terrifying head rising high above the waters, bearing him with it, and he called their orders down to them from his elevated position while one of his wizards amplified his voice.

He repeated a variation of the sermon he'd given Loch, to remind them of what they faced and what they stood to gain.

"These people need to cast off the dragon yoke that keeps them in misery. We must remind them of that and show them what they stand to gain. Without the dragon scourge gobbling resources with their big appetites and their foolish battles, this realm can know true prosperity. Go now and seek allies in the city. Bid them join arms with us against this tyranny."

A quick cheer rose from the men on the rafts, and then another gentle wave rolled them into the city. As the serpent brought Draxli back down to the water, he caught a glimpse of Loch looking at him approvingly. Turning a significant number of Pasdale's citizens would be crucial to keeping the boy on his side. He was young and still soft, but Draxli was confident that he would learn in time.

Now there was nothing to do but wait and steadily pour water into the city until dawn, when they would begin the final assault. Draxli would drive the Joasera women out of the city and bait their dragons into battle, preferring to leave the city intact. Once he had destroyed the enemy, his aquamancers could rapidly drain away the excess water. He envisioned stepping in to act as the saviour spearheading the cleanup.

He was startled out of his thoughts by the sounds of his dragons—all four of them in cataclysmic unison—screeching at an ear-splitting pitch that bowed him forward until his forehead touched the slimy back of his water beast. The beast itself shuddered, and he barely kept it from plunging beneath the water.

Tracking the horrific sound, he spotted his dragon allies floundering in the sky, slowly losing altitude at first, then plummeting. A wall of frigid air blasted Draxli an instant before the flailing dragons plunged into the waters, sloshing colossal waves around them. Draxli initially believed that his aquamancers had held the waves stationary, but then realized that the water where the dragons had splashed down had frozen entirely. To his horror, the ice spread from the point of impact.

"Loch!"

"M'lord, what's happening? What happened to the dragons?"

"You need to stop the ice."

"I—m'lord..." he stammered. "What do I...?"

"Lord Dunham," a calm voice enquired. His top elemental drew up in a raft alongside the serpent. "These dragons have been forsaken by their mother element. They have betrayed the fire realm by siding with your aquamancers. Their essence has been withdrawn."

"Reverse it."

The man bowed apologetically.

"It's not that simple, m'lord. The fire realm has retreated entirely from these dragons, stripping them of all heat. They should perish quickly, but we will be hard-pressed to stop the spread of the ice until they do. We will need fire—warmth—to undo this."

"Can't we fill them with a different element?" Loch asked. "Won't aeromancy help them? They fly."

"We've no dedicated aeromancers," the elemental said, "only aquamancers."

"Could we fill their essence with water?" Loch said.

"Let them die." Draxli shrugged, already growing bored.

"M'lord, the ice is spreading rapidly. I can keep our vessels back, but the city will be overwhelmed."

"Try the water, then. Or cut their misery short. It matters not to me, but do it quickly."

Draxli watched on, only half interested, as the elemental leapt to Loch's raft, all the while pushing the armada and Draxli's serpent away from the spreading ice. The raft disappeared on a rolling wave, one that continually built over the ice, freezing as fast as it travelled. The unnerving crackling of ice chased Draxli through the night, and he could only wait and watch as the water rapidly froze. At last, a triumphant screech echoed from the darkness.

The ice continued cracking, the night punctuated by its loud pops as the water reclaimed it. Then he heard snapping and snarling, the crashing pound of wings beating against the breaking ice around them. As the ice melted, Loch and the elemental slid back toward him, the four dragons staggering along behind them, sloshing through the icy water.

"They're still frozen."

"Yes, m'lord. The water essence is only sustaining them," the elemental said. "Loch did well for himself to negotiate the element transfer. But these dragons are forsaken by fire. Their cold no longer spreads beyond their bodies, insulated by the power of water, but their fires have forsaken them to the end of their days."

"Can they fight?" Draxli asked, losing interest.

"They will be able to eventually. But they are back in their infancy."

Draxli was tempted to dismiss the beasts entirely but saw the flash of intelligence in their eyes. Their minds had not suffered in the transition, even if their physical abilities were infantile.

"You can do no more to help this day," Draxli said to them. "Go, my friends, and build your strength for future battles."

He watched for only a moment as the dragons stumbled through the water, Loch parting it before them until they clambered over the hillside and out of sight, leaving a trail of frost in their wake. Then he turned back to Pasdale as the rafts drifted closer once more, the aquamancers swirling up a current to more rapidly break up the ice. There was nothing left to do but wait for the pyromancers and their dragons to appear.

The loss of Draxli's own dragons was inconvenient, but the power of his aquamancers was all he truly needed to end the battle. Pasdale would be his.

CHAPTER TWENTY

The battle for Pasdale raged and reports came into the Guild about the havoc wrought by the demons. Neesha only caught the snippets delivered to her mother, but it painted a grim picture. There had been no word yet from Ondias in the Red Mountains, but they didn't have many powerful wizards with them. It was unclear if any of them could send a message across such a distance.

Neesha was in the dragon chamber of the Guild, huddled on some cushions at the dragoness's side. She leaned against the great beast, taking comfort in her radiant heat and cradling Mita in her arms. Not even a makeshift bassinet had been found for the babe, but even if one had been presented, Neesha would be hard-pressed to put the child down.

Dionelle brought a chair to sit nearby, and the healer came in regularly to make sure Neesha took enough fluids, that she'd started to eat, that the babe was latching properly. If it wasn't the healer, it was Dionelle leaning in, checking on them both.

The dragoness, meanwhile, was silent, watching them all. Watching Mita. All the baby really did was sleep. So Neesha did plenty of the same. The dragoness slept when Neesha did, was awake when she was. The long journey and the trauma of losing the dragon city had exhausted them.

They rested, but they were not idle.

In other parts of the Guild, wizards were making plans to end the siege on Pasdale.

Tired as Neesha was, sleeping was difficult. Every movement, every whimper from the sleeping baby caught her attention.

She's mine.

It was impossible not to see that part of Neesha dwelled within her daughter. And she doubted it was only that they were both so visibly fireborn.

Neesha was perpetually dumbstruck by how this little human was here now, where there had been only Neesha before. Her breath caught in her chest and her mind tried to skitter away from the thoughts.

I'm a mother now.

And as much as Neesha hated sentimentality, she sank down into it, wallowed in it. She was a mother. She was Mita's mother. She'd never seen anything as beautiful as the little bundle in her arms. It was hard to breathe through the profound sense of love she felt. Fierce and protective.

The mantle of motherhood would not be easy, just as her own mother had warned all along. The responsibility was deep. Even as the baby turned Neesha's thoughts to warm goo, her spine filled with steel until she thought she could breathe fire.

Neesha looked up from her quiet contemplations when rapid footsteps echoed through the chamber. Nandara swept into the room, marching straight for them, her face ashen and her mouth pressed into a thin line.

"What's happened?" Dionelle stood as soon as she saw the look on Nandara's face.

"Lady Zyx was killed in the battle in Pasdale." Nandara kept her voice low. "It's not clear which side is responsible, but this is going to make things very difficult for us. Draxli's rhetoric has taken hold while we've been gone, and the lady's absence will only make our task more difficult."

"Is Draxli there?" Neesha asked.

"He is. His forces are concentrated in Pasdale, though they will be likely to switch their focus now that Lady Zyx has been eliminated."

"Then we go to Pasdale and we end him," Neesha said, fully expecting to see flames coming from her mouth. "My daughter will not be his victim."

"Do you have an idea?" Nandara asked. "You are still weak and should rest."

"There's no time. The portals are open and I want to use that while we can. Have you learned to control the energy from that realm?"

Nandara shook her head, getting paler.

Neesha looked to her mother. "Have you been able to wield any of it?"

"I tried, it pains me too much. My immunity isn't strong enough."

"Then I'll do it, and now. The risk is only mine, now that Mita is her own person. Mamma, you have to let me do this. Just promise me you will care for Mita if something goes wrong."

"Neesha, please—"

"Promise me!"

"Of course I will."

Neesha looked to the dragoness.

"Your family is kin to me," she said.

Neesha nodded, resolute, and carefully rose to her feet, Mita still cradled at her chest.

"We go to Pasdale now. With the portals from the fire realm still open, I can wield the fire to end Draxli and then use the demons to close the portals and send them back. I can do it. I'm the only one who can."

She turned to the dragoness, ignoring her mother's protests.

"I need you to send me back to the fire realm. I can take the portal there to Pasdale, it will be the quickest way."

"But the rest of us can't go with you," Dionelle said.

"You can," Neesha insisted. "The fire realm won't harm the three of us or any of the dragons."

"I will come with you," the dragoness said.

"All right," Dionelle said. "We can be quick, can't we?"

"We'll go quickly. Can the dragons send us back to the part of the realm where the portals are?"

"I believe they can," the dragoness said.

Still clutching Mita to her chest, Neesha slowly but purposely made her way out of the dragon chamber. No one tried to stop her.

She almost looked back to dare them to argue, but she already heard Nandara and her mother expanding on her plans, Nandara advising Dionelle on how to guide Neesha and promising to send a message to Zev so he could help them.

That was it? They were going to listen to her plan, just like that? The dragoness had already left, presumably to rally other dragons to the cause.

Making her deliberate way through the halls of the Guild, Neesha noticed all the wizards in her midst. Everyone was busy, all bustle and urgent chatter, but they nodded in her direction as she passed. No one treated her as an outsider.

She was one of them.

Maybe her entrance to the Guild was only temporary, but that would change. It would take some time, but she *would* properly belong to this Guild. She was already part of it, probably always had been. She saw that now. A smile tugged at the corners of her lips.

And maybe it wouldn't take so long to become a formal Guild member. Not when she would soon have Stone's support. His mother, her mother and grandmother. Many hands make easy work. Many hands to help care for Mita so Neesha could continue to grow.

They all knew she was only beginning to scratch the surface of what she could do as a pyromancer. What more could she do with training and time?

Her smile widened and she planted a kiss on her baby's smooth, soft head.

"Do you think all this will even be enough for Pa?"

Now *that* would be something.

She made it back outside to where the dragons were gathered. The black dragoness was already out there delivering the new terms to the Superiors. Dionelle caught up to Neesha outside the door, and they approached the dragons together.

The Dragoness Superior watched them with narrowed eyes, her body taut, but she remained silent as they gathered at the centre of the group. The black dragoness had come in behind Neesha and her mother, and Neesha turned to her.

"What's going on?"

"This is a dangerous endeavour. None of my kin will make the journey with us, though they give us their blessing."

"We have to take on all of Draxli's forces without dragons?" She tried and failed to keep her voice from rising.

"You will have my aid. And you have the ability to command the whole of the fire realm. Hope is not lost."

Neesha grit her teeth and faced forward, staring out into the gathered blaze of dragons. She held her breath in an attempt to still her trembling as the dragons began their spellcasting. A white hot wave washed over them, sending them back to the fire realm.

Neesha was re-energized by the fire, but Dionelle collapsed under the pain of the realm, exhausted after the night of helping Neesha bring Mita into the world. Neesha cried out in alarm, worried that this trip was even worse for Dionelle than the last. The dragoness scooped Dionelle up to carry her, although it was clear that she also struggled.

"Will this have consequences for you, Mistress?" Neesha asked.

"I do not care. It should not, but I will fly those skies when it comes."

"Help me however you can, but I can finish this on my own if I must." She turned to her mother. "Mamma, I want you to take Mita and watch her while I do this. I'm going to invoke a demon possession, and I want you keep an eye on things, in case it takes over me. The important thing is that you let me do whatever I must to destroy Draxli."

Dionelle scowled. They didn't have time to get Mita somewhere safer, but Neesha was confident in her mother's abilities.

They arrived in Pasdale through the fire in the massive hearth of the palace's hall where Neesha had taken her disastrous exam. It was all strangely silent and empty. Like a large, pretty mausoleum.

None of the adjoining hallways were large enough for the dragoness, and just as Neesha envisioned the creature trapped in the palace, the dragoness stretched on her hind legs, driving her claws through a dome of coloured glass above them. Neesha and Dionelle darted down the main hallway to protect themselves the falling shards.

With the glass ceiling destroyed, a torrent of water poured through the opening. The dragoness squeezed through to freedom.

As Neesha and Dionelle made their way through the castle, the only sounds were their bare feet slapping against the stone and the stampeding rain outside. No people milled about, no preparations for war being made.

"Do you think they're all outside trying to combat this devilry?" Neesha asked.

Dionelle shook her head. "We need to find a blanket for Mita," she said. "We need to know what's going on out there, and then we need to find a fire we can use. Zev is supposed to meet us in the dragon chamber."

"Good, let's see if your dragoness is waiting for us. She may have seen the battle."

The dragoness was, indeed, waiting for them in the dragon chamber. Dionelle called out in delight when she saw that Zev was there as well. He stood quietly next to the dragoness, both of them watching the doorway, waiting for their arrival. Neesha let out a long breath, hoping they'd get some answers. She wanted to be fully prepared to battle the water this time.

"I received Nandara's message. How can I help?"

"I need a fire outside," Neesha said. "Is there anywhere near the city where the rain won't touch our fire?"

Zev frowned and closed his eyes. "You would have to go to the edge of the valley, like you did the first time. Unless one of the towers would work for you? Some of them have top-floor rooms with windows on all sides. With the glass broken out you could send fire out into the battle but still have the roof for protection."

"Yes, a tower is perfect. One near the north."

"Has Draxli released water demons?" Dionelle asked. "Have they opened a water portal?"

"If water demons are involved, they haven't come into the city yet. But a water portal makes the most sense considering the sheer amount of water we're seeing in such a short time. The situation has become complicated." Zev looked to the dragoness, his expression concerned and apologetic. "There are far too many people swayed by Draxli's words who believe him when he says that the dragons are responsible for this, particularly for the loss of Lady Zyx. That she drowned makes no difference. The fire demons loose in the city do not help us combat Draxli's words."

Neesha looked from the dragoness to Zev, not seeing the problem.

"People from the city—including some of our own soldiers—have been attacking the dragons here trying to help us. Many of the dragons have abandoned the cause."

"One dragon is all we need," Neesha said. "She won't abandon us. Be sure to have your guards protecting her."

"Do you know who Draxli has controlling the water?" Dionelle asked. "He must have a whole host of aquamancers in his midst."

"He has five of the most powerful elementals I've ever encountered. Nandara was able to help identify them—one of them even a former student of hers."

"I need to know how to find them," Neesha said.

"They stay close to Draxli. He is currently out in the flooded northern fields on the back of a great water beast the likes of which none of us has ever seen."

"Take me to a tower on the northern side of the castle," Neesha said. "I will reduce Draxli and his beast to ash."

Zev tilted his head, brows arching. "The fire demons have helped a great deal to push back the water—they have been drawing on phenomenal power from their realm, but we need to reign them in. They have destroyed large sections of the city with fires—people are terrorized."

"I will control them and send them where they're needed," Neesha said. "Once Draxli is dead, I will close the portals and the demons will be pulled back to their realm."

Neesha turned to Dionelle, but looked down at the precious bundle she carried. For the first time since Mita was born, Neesha let someone else hold her, pressing the babe into Dionelle's arms. Even as she did so, Neesha couldn't meet her mother's gaze, couldn't pry her eyes from her child. Dionelle cooed at her granddaughter. Neesha felt heavy and empty all at once. Her lungs had gone to stone.

"Mamma." She forced herself to breathe. "Take care of Mita, but stay with me, all right?"

Dionelle looked at her with shining eyes and nodded. "I'll find some blankets for her, and maybe some boots for us. I will meet you in the tower."

Dionelle, who was familiar with the castle, left on her own while Zev escorted Neesha out of the dragon chamber. They retraced the route she'd taken with Dionelle almost all the way back to the large dining hall, where water still cascaded through the destroyed dome. Zev kept going, turning away from the hall, and Neesha recognized the corner of the palace they'd entered. It was a wide corridor between the main entrance and what until very recently had been Lady Zyx's throne room.

As Zev turned down a side corridor, a familiar voice called to Neesha. She stopped in her tracks.

"Neesha, wait!" Stone called.

She turned from Zev to see Stone breaking away from an escort guard, the first people she'd seen since finding Zev. Stone rushed toward her.

"What the devil are you doing here?" she asked, both of them skipping formalities as Stone folded her into his arms.

Zev walked ahead a few paces, giving the pair some space.

"All this fire, I knew it had to be you," he said. "When I saw that dragoness come in the palace, I knew you'd be here."

"Why are you here? Why aren't you with River and Ember?"

"The flooding came too fast this time. I had to seek shelter with a friend near the eastern temple."

"You should have stayed there." Neesha pulled from his embrace. "It's too dangerous out on the streets."

"I was cautious. I feared this would be my last opportunity to see you."

She smiled wryly. "I am protected by these castle walls and by a dragoness. And that's to say nothing of my own power. I'm going up to the tower to open gates directly to the fire realm."

"Like you did last time."

"Yes, but this time I have nothing to hold me back." She pressed his hand over her belly, still larger than normal but soft. "Her name is Mita. She's with my mother, and I'm free to call on demons for aid and the very realm itself for strength. It will be different."

Stone smiled at her, but it was a sad smile. He drew her close to him, squeezing her.

"You'll end it this time. I know you will. Don't hold back," he said, surprising her. "I don't like that you're the only one who can save Pasdale, but I know you'll do it right."

He paused, his smile fading with the sadness. He touched her hair and stroked her cheek.

"You do what you need to. Stop this like only you can. The gods know someone must—the city is drowning. I'll understand if you don't come back."

"I'll come back. And I'll keep my promise. The dragoness can fetch my family and I'll find you with your friend. Good that he's near a temple, makes it easier for us."

His smile returned and he kissed her forehead.

"But…" She paused, not wanting to consider the possibility. But she had to. Dionelle often criticized Neesha for thinking only of herself, but what was Mita if not an extension of her? "But if it goes wrong, if I don't come back. Will you do what you can for Mita? I hope that my family will accept her, that my father will soften to her. But if he doesn't…"

"I will always treat Mita as my own."

She nodded, surprised at how much lighter she felt. She squeezed his hand.

"Now go," she said, her voice stern and uncompromising. "Get back to that friend of yours. Quickly. Stay under cover. It's going to get wild here very soon."

He nodded and turned away, disappearing back down the hall. Once she was certain Stone was actually going to seek cover, she rejoined Zev. Without comment, he led her through the building and up the tower stairs. Neesha had a hard time keeping up with him, her very soul seemed to ache after all that had happened in the past week. She couldn't make her body move any faster. The very idea of all the upcoming spellcraft she'd have to perform—and the toll it would take—made her weary body feel even heavier.

She would have to draw enough energy directly from the fire realm. It was a terrible long-term strategy, but she only needed energy enough to get through the day. It was time to end this battle.

CHAPTER
TWENTY-ONE

The room at the top of the northern tower was some sort of observatory, with wide, floor-to-ceiling windows spaced by narrow stone supports little wider than the bookshelves and storage cupboards that lined them. She tried not to notice the grey wall of rain beyond the windows, or the insidious dark blotch of encroaching floodwaters beyond.

But that she could see so much meant this would be the perfect place to make her stand. To take down Draxli and end his foolishness. To safeguard this stupid valley... Her stupid valley. And to keep her family safe—the one she'd always known and the little one she was starting for herself. She thought briefly of Stone, hoped he was safely indoors.

She'd be his wife soon enough. It didn't terrify her like it used to. It helped to remember that she didn't have to *keep* being his wife. And that she didn't have to be his wife in any traditional sense if she didn't want to.

But those were thoughts for later. For now, she needed fire.

Neesha walked directly to the nearest bookshelf and indiscriminately tossed the books into the middle of the room, trying to ignore her body's protestations at the work. She'd been warned about how taxing the birth would be, but everything that had come before it, heaped on top of the expectations of the moment, certainly weren't helping.

When this was over she was going to sleep for an entire month.

Once she'd cleared the shelf of books, she toppled it, splintering off a few pieces that she added to the pile in the middle. By the time she began repeating the process with a second shelf, Zev caught on to her intention, and he dragged the remains of the first shelf to the centre of the room, stomped on it to break it apart and created a base for a bonfire. He cracked the books' spines so they would lay open and crumpled their pages, tenting the wood around them with plenty of space for air to flow. Together, Neesha and Zev took apart the second bookshelf and built a large pile in the middle of the room.

As they finished, Dionelle returned wearing the swaddled baby in a wrap—partially hidden under her cloak, and wearing ill-fitting boots. She brought Neesha a pair that fit as poorly as her own, but they would do.

The pile in the middle of the room would sustain the kind of fire Neesha needed. It was time to get started. She picked up an iron rod, formerly ornamentation on one of the shelves, and smashed out the windows facing north.

She couldn't see much through the wall of rain, but that was of little consequence. The black dragoness stopped circling the city and flew straight for the tower once the smashed out windows caught her attention. She blasted in more windows with her tail, and then carefully perched on the roof of the tower, leaning down to peer in. She glared at Zev.

"There's fire coming," Neesha said to him. "You should go. Find somewhere safe."

He glanced at Dionelle and then slipped out the door and back down the stairs. Dionelle moved to the doorway, backing away from the coming fire. Neesha stood clear, preferring not to lose the boots she'd only just acquired as the dragoness shot flame into the centre of the room, lighting the books and wood that Zev and Neesha had arranged there.

The bonfire was massive in the enclosed space, even with the room's vaulted ceilings. Smoke billowed and the acrid stench filled her nose, chasing out the damp smell of the unending rain.

Neesha walked to where the dragoness was perched and lay her hand on the beast's great muzzle.

"This will get ugly very soon and I fear for all three of us. I know you will help however you can, but for now, I need your fires near Draxli. You will be my guide so I can reach him with demonflame," Neesha said. "Wait for me to gather the demons and push back the rains, then seek him out so that I can end this."

"Shall I take a demon into me?" the dragoness asked.

"Do you believe that to be wise?"

"There is no wisdom in any of this," the dragoness replied, her dark eyes glittering. "But that does not make it less necessary."

"I will send you a demon then. Be strong, my friend, and may the winds that carry you be blessed."

The dragoness snorted out a playful line of fire, its tendrils curling around Neesha's face. Then the great beast took flight, circling the tower and waiting for Neesha to act. Neesha reported her plan to her mother, kissing Dionelle and Mita on the forehead for luck. Her gaze lingered on the tiny, vulnerable bundle of her baby secured to her mother. Neesha's throat tightened, but she forced a breath through and turned from them.

The fire's heat called to her. She strode to its edge, standing just far enough back it didn't burn her boots, and let the power of fire fill her like gusts of dry prairie wind at the height of summer. Tension melted from her body, and a great centre of calm spread out before her.

She summoned the demons, calling them from the city streets to the tower, filling the room with their intense light. There were far more of them than she had anticipated, and outside of their realm, she had a tenuous grip on their language. She sent one to the dragoness, but couldn't convince others to resume their attacks on the water.

But summoning them hadn't been difficult, and allowing possession wasn't either. She'd wanted to avoid it. If only she had Nandara with her.

"Mamma, do you speak their language?"

Neesha glanced at the doorway where Dionelle was pressed against the wall, trembling, one arm shielding her eyes from the intense light.

"No. Not anymore." Her voice held the same tremor.

"Can you control them at all?"

"One at a time."

Even with the two of them working together, the city would drown before they could coax all of the demons back into the fight. They had to try.

"That's a start," Neesha said. "Send them out to fight the water. We need to burn it away."

Neesha plucked a demon from her midst, calling to it like she had so many times when practicing at home. It came, like they always did, crackling heat washing over her. Her head swam with it. She was giddy. Unstoppable.

She took a deep breath and focused her thoughts, turning away from the mischief the demon was intent on. Gripping the creature with her will, she granted it enough reign over her that she could command the other demons.

The thoughts in her mind did not match the sounds that issued forth from her, the demon converting her intentions to commands the other demons understood. *Now* she spoke their language.

The demons burst forth from the tower, roiling across the sky as she had seen them do once before.

No longer caring about her boots or the broken glass nearby, Neesha walked further into the flame where the demons' power was at its strongest. It was far simpler than she anticipated to link this fire to the one in the keep where she had already opened a gate to the fire realm, giving herself unlimited access to firepower.

Giving the demon inside her a little more freedom allowed her to connect to any demon in battle that she chose. Now she could see through the eyes of the possessed dragoness as she closed in on a great host in the waters beyond the city. Half Neesha's mind dizzied at the effect of her vision swooping through the air while her feet remained firmly planted on the tower floor.

The other half of her mind had been given over to the demon, and it was focused on fire.

Some of Draxli's people rode beasts like Draxli did. Many others were in boats and on rafts, buoyed by sympathetic waters that would drown all their foes. Demon fire drove back the water all around, boiling it into mist that was nearly impossible for human eyes to see through.

Neesha was no longer seeing through human eyes.

She floated in raw power, a volcano come to life. Heat and fury coursed through her like molten lava. It buoyed her. She drew deep from within the fire realm, energized. The act was as simple as pulling heat from any normal fire.

Her fractured mind spun, trying to comprehend the sheer power she could access. And control.

She grinned, full of teeth and flames.

Pulling on that endless supply, she funnelled precise columns of fire from her hands. With the simplest gestures, she directed it to the battle ahead of her, like plucking strings on a lute to weave a melody.

Through the dragoness's demon, she spotted Draxli on his water beast, a great snakelike creature roiling near the surface. Seeing him broiled her in white hot fury. Scorching hatred for the man who had once terrorized her parents and now sought to destroy all that she loved.

There were aquamancers in boats around him. She directed the columns of fire there next, while the demons continued to boil away the host's water. As the water heated around it, the great water beast bucked and twisted, nearly throwing Draxli from its back.

The power coursing through her tugged at her, pulling forward. A spooked horse trying to bolt. Still grinning, but contorted with the effort, Neesha grit her teeth and strained against the power, feeling it sear. She shuddered. Pain from fire?

She had no time to consider what it meant. The power would slip and she needed to finish this before it could. She clamped down on the energy and focused it once more.

Through the dragoness's demon, Neesha burned away the boats carrying the aquamancers, not caring if their waters saved them or they were boiled alive or drowned. She blasted them with columns of fire, spinning and spiralling with devastating beauty.

It took her breath away.

But she held her focus, one arm thrust out as she saw through the dragoness. One blazing column, so bright neither she nor the dragoness could look directly at it, twisted into Draxli's beast.

The light burst like ten thousand suns, lasting only a moment but incinerating the creature as she had sworn she would. Draxli was tossed free before it could take him.

Rage sizzled through her mind like white hot lightning. She would not lose him.

But her grip on the power slipped. She screamed against it. Or at least it felt like a scream. The roar of fire and power was so great she heard nothing else.

She let go of all of the demons and their power. She didn't need it. She released all but two: the one she possessed and the one in the dragoness. Everything snapped back into focus.

It felt like a stretched eternity as Neesha watched through the dragoness's intense scrutiny while Draxli tumbled through the air, tracking him as he flipped end over end. She pulled hard on the demon in the dragoness. Her focus narrowed down to the tiniest pinprick. All of her being condensed to that one moment.

Through the demon, she could control the dragoness. But Neesha didn't have to. The dragoness dived from the air, plunging into the waters. She snatched Draxli from any respite he may hope to find there, gripping him in her teeth.

Neesha was so connected to the demons and their rampage that she felt Draxli's body giving way under the dragoness's mighty jaws. Bones snapped like kindling. Flesh tore like paper. At last, the dragoness tossed him out into the growing conflagration. Pieces of him fell through the fire; his ashes rained down into the water.

Neesha screamed in triumph.

The sound mingled with the demon language and a primal scream in her own voice. She balled her hands into fists, thrusting them victoriously into the air.

Draxli and his aquamancers were gone.

Neesha had never felt so powerful in her life. Like a mighty sun unto herself, burning bright. The pain of all that power seared, electrifying every nerve ending until she went numb. But she held control. She would put it to good use.

There was so much water left, even as the clouds melted away and the sun shone through for the first time in far too many days. The fields of Pasdale were soaked beyond reckoning, the entire valley submerged. With a direct link to demon power from the fire realm, Neesha could burn away the remaining deluge. She could dry out the fields so men like Stone could work. Fields like Stone's and her family's and so many other families.

But she had to focus. Draxli was gone—the threat he had created was not.

While she held control, Neesha reached deep into the realm of fire and pulled up a massive blazing column. As she thrust her hands out, the fire thundered over the city and out into the battle beyond.

Even over the blaze crackling around her, Neesha heard water sizzling, a great roar of clashing elements. She bit down harder, squeezing her eyes as she strained to hold on. She was the conduit. Arms spread, she poured more and more energy from the fire realm into the spellwork.

She pushed her gaze back into the dragoness, watching as the waters receded into great clouds in the sky. Those clouds raced away on the winds to disperse the water across the kingdom and out to the seas where it belonged.

Time no longer had meaning, and Neesha had no way of knowing how much of it had passed while she'd driven fire out into the water, boiling it away. But her mother was at her side.

"Neesha, you have to close the gate!"

Neesha barely understood her words, had no recollection of what gate her mother spoke of. From the fire's core she glanced over to where Dionelle stood cautiously at the edge of the fire. She wasn't sure why Dionelle stayed so far back, why she wouldn't join her when the fire would do little more than burn away the boots she wore.

"Neesha, hear me," Dionelle commanded, a different kind of fire in her voice.

More orders. Neesha was tired of orders. Especially from her mother. When she had power like this, she didn't need orders. Neesha turned away.

"Neesha Autumn Joasera, hear me!"

Neesha stopped like she'd reached the end of a rope. She turned without knowing why. But nothing was more important than her mother's words.

"The demon has taken you," Dionelle said. "Push it out, reclaim yourself, and close the gate to the fire realm before the demons burn away the entire world."

The woman's fear held Neesha's attention for a moment, but she couldn't see why she needed to let the power go. She could do so much more.

She began turning away to unleash as much fire on her enemies as she could pull from the realm. But then she saw little Mita, only hours old. A fragile little thing, sleeping peacefully in her swaddle, safe in her grandmother's arms.

Safe. But only for now.

The gates could not be left open indefinitely, or they would have the same effect on the balance of nature that a human's presence in the fire realm would. If Neesha meant to protect her daughter, she would have to close the gates.

The power turned bitter. She gasped, nearly choked.

But she'd come too far to fail now.

She let some of the power slip. She didn't need much for what she had to do.

Neesha summoned demons once more and ushered them through the gates. She stretched her thoughts to the gates in the fire realm—all three of them—and pulled them closed, one by one. The gate to Pasdale snapped shut last. As it closed, the unimaginable energy she had released was pulled back in.

Some of the demons went with it, a great helix of light.

The power surged through her. But it caught in her mind, tugging as it went, dragging her back to the fire realm with it. Pain tore at her like her body was coming apart. She grasped at anything around her, but there was nothing but heat and light. It was like swimming against rapids. She caught a glimpse of her mother with arms outstretched, the little bundle of Mita nestled in her firecloak, and then only a wall of fire.

As the final gate to the fire realm shut tight, intense light beyond reckoning consumed all vision and thought.

EPILOGUE

Dionelle had scarcely left the little outcropping next to the shimmering diamond base of the western support column. She barely noticed the glittering red mountainside or the gleam of the column rising next to her or the remnants of the dragon city that clung to the remaining three columns. Her gaze focused only on Neesha entombed within the column, sustained by the scant magic the dragons still possessed. It was old magic and would linger as long as the beasts remained, but it provided small comfort.

Her daughter was lost to her, dreaming her visions of fire and victory, locked in a single moment on the outermost edge of life. Dionelle had felt certain, after the city fell and Neesha truly took the threat seriously, that she would escape the fate she'd made for herself. That history would not repeat itself. That Dionelle would not lose her daughter the way she'd lost her sister.

And while selflessness rather than selfishness had been Neesha's undoing, the result was the same. They had merely taken a different path to the same place. Would Mita escape such a fate?

It was hard to say how long Neesha would stay in this state, if she would ever wake or if she would slip fully into death at any moment. The dragons seemed to have an idea, and they didn't seem especially concerned, but without voices, it was difficult to understand what they meant.

Dionelle had not been able to speak through her grief, and it seemed the dragons had similarly lost their voices. She couldn't say if it was an act of empathy, of mourning on their part, or if there was some deep magic at work. Neesha's encroachment on the fire realm had inextricably linked the dragons' power to the fate of the fireborn women.

It was Ondias, of course, who came with the black dragoness to collect Dionelle from the mountainside. Lost in her mourning, Dionelle didn't notice Ondias at first, didn't realize she was no longer alone until the black dragoness gently nudged her shoulder with her great, soft muzzle. The warm touch of the creature soothed Dionelle's grief, even if only for a moment.

Even after all these years, Dionelle remained surprised by how soft the dragoness was to the touch, even though she had handled dragon skin plenty of times. The last time had been when she folded her daughter's amethyst cloak and stored it away for Mita to use when she was older, or for Neesha, should she ever be restored to them.

Dionelle affectionately patted the dragoness's muzzle and gave her an appreciative look before turning to Ondias.

"You know you can't stay," Ondias said.

Dionelle looked away, looking back to where Neesha rested so peacefully.

"I'll be here, you know that."

Dionelle gave Ondias a sharp gaze, shaking her head almost imperceptibly.

Ondias bristled. "Don't give me that look. I don't care what happens in Pasdale anymore. My duty is here."

Dionelle watched her. Did she really mean that?

"The children love it here with me. Zev will come around. There's nothing good left for him in the court anyway."

Dionelle sighed and turned away. She couldn't imagine that Zev would ever agree to this arrangement, but there was no talking Ondias out of her current magical thinking.

"Don't give me that! The children will come here. Zev will or he won't. I'm staying." Ondias sat next to her, looking at Neesha. "I'll watch over her and I'll send her straight home if she wakes."

Dionelle nodded, knowing all this was true. She wondered if it would be wise to send Neesha home directly. It might be better for Dionelle to return to the dragon city.

Of course, Ondias was a bright woman and she would see that quickly enough, if she didn't already. Ondias herself, after all, was not returning to Pasdale, and she was apparently convinced that once Zev untangled himself from service under Pasdale's regency council, he would collect their children and join her in the Red Mountains. In any case, Ondias was clearly intent on staying in the dragon city.

Dionelle wondered if she could convince Reiser that the entire family was better off with the dragons. As Nandara had feared, Draxli's words had poisoned opinions, and too few people knew the truth of what had happened. The demon rampage was blamed on the dragons, and the final victory was seen as belonging solely to Neesha. Many blamed the dragons for Neesha's death.

Of course, she wasn't actually dead, but there was no way to dispel the rumours when she wasn't exactly alive, either.

"It's getting late," Ondias said gently. "You should take some rest and prepare for tomorrow."

Dionelle sighed, ambivalent about the coming journey. She would be relieved to return to the comforts of home and the reassurance of Reiser's arms. It would be good to see the baby and the boys again. But she felt she was abandoning Neesha in the rock, alone.

Alone maybe, but certainly not forgotten. There had been a constant vigil from the dragons, even as they strove to rebuild their city. Nandara had found a terramancer, one of the best the world had to offer, to help her team of elementals raise the mountain on the north side of the valley so that the dragons could resurrect the city's support structures. Still, it could take as much as a decade to fully restore the mountain.

Dionelle looked out into the valley and watched the dragons industriously collecting the shattered pieces of their city and carrying them out to the remaining columns, fusing obsidian to obsidian and diamond to diamond, building new arches out over the valley.

The human settlement was stationed at the southern pass for now, the rubble from the collapse blocking any hope of rebuilding their shelters just yet. Still, there were many tents erected on the ground, the human contingent quite large—all of them had been there when the city had been destroyed, and none of them would leave. Those most loyal to the dragons were migrating out to the Red Mountains to offer their help where they could.

The Wizards Guild, of course, would fulfill its promise of aid to the dragons, which was why Nandara and her comrades were there working the earth to raise the mountain again. They had to be cautious, though, not to raise the ire of an angry kingdom—rightfully angry—but full of misdirected blame. The death of Lady Zyx heralded an end to a golden age for Pasdale and many of the surrounding regions.

The dragoness nudged her, and Dionelle turned to see the creature watching her intently, head tilted impatiently. Dionelle smiled and nodded, consenting to being brought back down into the valley to rest and prepare for the journey home.

Idleness would not serve Neesha. And Dionelle had a granddaughter to think of.

Scan here or visit thodestool.ca/news to learn more about Vanessa's work or to sign up for her newsletter.

FIREBORN SERIES BOOK THREE

A SNEAK PEEK

CHAPTER ONE

Spark Joasera had less than an hour to find a present for her cousin's birthday, and every shiny thing in the market called out to her. Most of it was inaccessible by either price or vendors who refused to serve her family. Spark eyed the tables strewn with bright fabric or glittering baubles, jars of spices, delicate herbs hanging from poles, fine cuts of meat, the baskets of fresh produce—both basic staples and rarities grown under glass domes—and the very best baked goods, piles of cakes, breads, buns and pastries, the rich scents making her wish they weren't rushing to pick up a few last minute items before heading home to make Bren's birthday dinner. But she didn't look at the merchants. She trudged along behind her grandmother, who knew all the most delicate intricacies of local politics. She knew who was safe.

Nanny Di led her deeper into the maze of tables and tents, passed a blacksmith with blades Spark dearly wanted to linger over, to admire the workmanship and wonder how she'd improve it. But even the tiniest dagger, little more than a decoration, was far beyond her means.

Spark paused beyond the blacksmith's corner and opened up her coin purse. She sighed and rushed to catch up with Nanny, who hadn't noticed her stop.

"Nanny, do you think any of the blacksmiths would take me as an apprentice—"

Nanny jerked to a halt and gave Spark a wide-eyed look over her shoulder.

"Come on, there's got to be one of them who will see the benefit of a fireproof assistant."

Nanny blinked once, her jaw tight. She shook her head and kept going, Spark hurrying to keep up.

"Not one? There's got to be one! Nanny, we need the money."

Nanny shook her head again but wouldn't even look at Spark now. It was always like this when Spark brought up finding something outside of their homestead for her to do. Not that she really needed an apprenticeship, the quality of her work was already outstanding. Didn't matter how brilliant she was if everyone would rather see her wares reduced to slag than buy them.

And she already had an apprenticeship with Nanny's friend Nandara, learning more about magic so she could become a full member of the Wizards Guild. She'd been a member under the specialist tiers for pyromancy since she was twelve, the earliest they'd let her take the exam—making her the youngest member to date—but full membership would allow her greater options.

Well, it would if anyone would so much as look at her, let alone talk to her or work with her.

She was sixteen, and recently done school, and she needed *something* to do with herself other than study magic. Her grandfather insisted they didn't need the money and she was more help out in the fields with him, but she didn't want to be a farmer. She needed more.

But it took all of them to keep the farm running, now that they didn't get outside help. She couldn't bear the thought of letting them down, so she sighed and continued to trudge through the market behind Nanny.

Nanny gathered a few quick supplies from locals and then headed to the travelling caravans. Unlike locals, these people talked with them, were friendly, and gave them fair prices without any haggling. Of course, Nanny haggled anyway, which was a delight for Spark to watch.

This time, it was with an academic Nanny knew. She found a book she wanted, something out of the dragon city by the way it was quickly wrapped up and tucked out of sight. Nanny always looked for new information about the dragons, things from far flung places, or the scholars studying them in the dragon city itself. Information untainted by Magistrate Loch's twisted words.

The academic gave Nanny the price, ten pennies. Nanny raised an eyebrow and didn't move, scrutinizing the man. He smiled shrewdly and offered her nine pennies for the book. The corners of Nanny's lips flickered up, and she counted out six pennies in front of him. He offered her eight. Nanny remained silent as the hills. And so it went until the man chuckled, rolled his eyes and took the six pennies.

While he spoke to Nanny, Spark heard familiar derisive laughter from a few tables over. She tried to ignore it but her traitor gaze landed on the group of whispering girls watching her and Nanny. Sight of their ringleader nearly made Spark's heart stop.

Janny with the glossy black hair that swayed down to her waist. Janny who more floated than walked. Janny who had always stayed out of the gossip, who had been almost kind to Spark, right up until a few weeks before school ended. Her stomach twisted. Janny used to make her stomach fizzy, but now it was more like the fizz was on fire.

"And this is Mita, is it?" The man glanced at Spark and she refocused on the conversation.

The nickname had been well earned, but Spark's mother had named her Mita after the patron saint of dragons.

"Hello, sir."

"You look so much like your mother." He smiled.

"Um, thanks."

Having never seen an image of Neesha as an adult, she had no idea if this was a compliment or not. But Nanny smiled, even if her eyes were sad. Spark got one side of her lips to curl up.

Spark had seen an old portrait of Nanny from the days before she married Pappy, when Nanny's power had been different and she'd been almost as white as Spark. Spark was like snow in the moonlight. Her skin and hair so white it nearly shone. Her eyes were rich liquid fire, amber through and through. Nanny was still thin as a whip, but her hair—shot through with silver—was rich and dark like coffee, pulled into a tight braid. Nanny's blue eyes held a flash of fire now and then, but the physical manifestation of her power had faded.

Nanny's smile drooped at the corners, and she ran her fingers through Spark's tangle of short hair. Spark kept it shorn down, like a little sheep.

Then Nanny wrapped one arm around Spark in a side-hug, upset as she often was at the mention of Spark's mother, Neesha.

Nanny Di got a face full of chest when she hugged Spark, not that Spark was particularly well endowed in that regard. She was broad like her grandfather but lean like her grandmother, and the tallness, well maybe that came from her father. Spark didn't know anything about him. None of them did. But her height together with the fireborn complexion she'd inherited from her mother left Spark looking like a long piece of parchment.

The man slid out from behind his table to give Nanny a hug, but Spark noticed him slipping a scroll to Nanny as he did. She wondered who it was from. Someone in the dragon city, likely Nanny's best friend, Ondias. From what Spark overheard from the adults, Nanny sometimes got messages from actual dragons. She didn't know why, but it made her uncomfortable.

Spark had met dragons, long ago before she'd started school. She had the vaguest remembrance of it. Fuzzy portraits of memory, like scenes from long ago dreams. They didn't seem real—no one saw dragons anymore. Not in Pasdale. Not wild dragons. Rarely captive ones either.

Nanny slipped the message into her pocket so quickly Spark wouldn't have known she had anything if she didn't already know about the practice. It was no danger to Nanny, or at least no more than there already was, for her to receive the banned messages from her friends in the dragon city, but any merchants found passing her the scrolls would face sanctions.

When there were enough wizards out in the dragon city, they magicked their messages to Nanny and saved the merchants the trouble.

Nanny smiled at the man, a hand over her heart. She gave him a quick wave and then motioned with her head for Spark to follow her. They continued on, Nanny collecting another book at another vendor, this one not someone she knew.

And then Spark saw it. A whole cart full of rubbish metal scraps. It was perfect. She snagged Nanny's cloak to stop her before she bustled on past.

It was a tinker's cart, of course. He had all manner of wonderful things that weren't broken trash that other people were more interested in. But Spark wanted to take his entire junk pile with her. Just give him her soul for the cart. She had only a few pennies, whatever Uncle Breen had been able to spare. She hoped it would do.

Nanny's hand fell on Spark's shoulder, breaking her reverie. Nanny had her head tilted to one side, a half smile as she appraised Spark. She raised one eyebrow.

"Yes, for Bren, I know. But I can make him something." Spark buzzed with an even better idea. "I can *show him* how to make something. We can make it together. Nanny, it's perfect!"

Nanny's smile grew and her hand moved from Spark's shoulder to her face. Then she gestured toward the cart and Spark bounced over and started poking through the pieces. Couldn't take it all, so she had to find something *just right*.

The tinker chatted idly with Spark while she looked through his supplies.

"Anything I can help you with?" he asked.

"I'll know when I see it." She smiled politely, hoped it would signal to him that she knew what she was doing. Sometimes they didn't trust her. She wasn't the only girl who could handle a forge, but it was rare enough she usually had to explain herself.

This tinker, thankfully, held out his hands in a placating gesture and let her look. Bent utensils, half a pitchfork, the corner of a plow, a dull axe blade. And then she found two matching scrap iron rods. Even with bartering, they cost all her pennies, and she was certain the tinker was giving them to her out of pity. She hadn't been able to hide the grin when she found them.

She tucked them into Nanny Di's pack and they continued on.

"Di! Spark! Wait."

They'd reached the edge of the city, but Spark recognized the voice and stopped immediately. Nandara, a powerful elemental wizard and Spark's mentor, rushed toward them. Spark had a lesson with her yesterday and was surprised to see her again so soon. Her grey-blonde hair flared out behind her as she strode forward, green eyes flashing. Her grey wizarding robes billowed around her medium build and she stopped in front of them, a bit taller than Nanny but nowhere near as tall as Spark.

"What a relief to catch you. I thought I'd have to make the trip out to you." She touched Nanny's shoulder and smiled at Spark, the rush to catch up with them flushing pink into her pale cheeks. "How are you today?"

"It's just always the same." This usually drew a smile from Nandara, but the one already on her face froze and her eyes scrunched.

"I haven't got a lot of time right now, but I'd like you to come by tomorrow so we can finish up with your apprenticeship."

"Finish?" Spark's mouth fell open. She should have at least two more years of intense study. Nandara couldn't possibly be thinking of putting her through her full Guild exams already. She'd never pass.

"I'm sorry, Spark. We'll need to go through some things so I can get you set to finish your studies on your own. With Dionelle's oversight of course."

"But..." Spark shook her head and appealed to Nanny, who stared at Nandara, her head tilted, with an expectant look on her face.

"I know this is sudden, but Riz finally agrees that it's time to go."

Riz was Nandara's husband, recently retired from Loch's court. Nandara was a court wizard but had been slowly reducing her role for years. She had been teaching Spark almost as long as Nanny had, even though the family couldn't pay her. She was one of the first people Nanny had befriended upon moving to Pasdale when she wed Pappy.

Spark helped Nandara with chores as much as she could, to try to make it even. Nandara had mentored Spark's mother, too, and Pappy said she'd have mentored Spark for nothing even if they had the money to pay her. Not just out of loyalty, but because she felt guilty. That she should have been able to prepare Neesha for the battles that eventually consumed her.

"We're packing now," Nandara said. "We plan to leave first thing in the morning come week's end. We leave for the Guild first. I've got some business there. We want to visit Sharanda, but we'll eventually make our way to the dragon city to be with Jatten. We want to get there while the mountains are still passable. It's a little late for that, of course, but now Riz thinks the new king will have some ridiculous travel taxes. He wants to be beyond the reach of Golden Hill before that happens."

Spark shook her head through the explanation, not liking any of it for an instant. Nandara was their connection to the world outside. The only friend they had left. So many of them left Pasdale ages ago to be closer to the dragons or farther from Magistrate Loch—or both.

Nanny was far too still and her face was pinched, her jaw clenched, like she'd stepped on a sharp rock and didn't want to cry out. She nodded slowly and shallowly so it was nearly imperceptible. Spark tried to parse what

Nandara said, trying to find what had Nanny so troubled. The adults often spoke in code. The words themselves weren't alarming, but the concern in each woman's face and the intensity of Nandara's quiet voice said more than Spark would ever know.

The new king in Golden Hill had been there for over a moon, she'd heard, but the news travelled to Pasdale slowly and they'd only known for a week. But the adults spoke about it plenty. Always with these looks and strange undertones.

Lost in thought and watching wagons clatter past, Spark missed some of what Nandara said.

"...will be dangerous," she whispered. This caught Spark's attention. "We can't wait. I'm so sorry. You really should make plans too."

Nandara noticed Spark watching them and forced a smile, turning her attention.

"Why don't you come with me? I can continue your lessons and you can see the Guild. They'd be delighted to have you back."

Spark started to correct her, that she'd never been to the Wizards Guild, and then she remembered. It had been a long time since anyone had mentioned, but Spark was born there. In the dragon chamber, if Pappy's wine-fuelled evening tales were to be believed.

"Then you don't have to cut your studies short," Nandara continued. "You can meet some other wizards, learn things books and Di's kitchen can never teach you. See the dragon city again. There are plenty of other apprentices there, from all sorts of trades, some of them your age or nearly so, like my grandson. Do you remember the dragon city?"

Spark shook her head. Like the dragons themselves, it was merely a vague notion. One that made little sense. She couldn't tell what was real memory and what was pure fancy wrought by story and imagination.

This wasn't the first time Nandara had tried, with Nanny's acquiescence, to convince Spark to come with her on her travels. Sometimes they talked about Spark going to live with Nanny's extended family to the south beyond Pasdale. This felt different. Spark wasn't sure if it was because Nandara was leaving for good. If Spark went, how would she get back? The dragon city was half the world away. And even if she knew the things Loch said about dragons were lies, the uncertainty and fear were hard to let go of. Especially when she couldn't properly remember dragons.

The two iron rods poked out of Nanny's bag, and Spark's stomach felt like it was full of ice. The thought of leaving filled her with dread. She didn't want Nandara to go. Nothing about this seemed right. But this was something different, something more. Maybe something she needed?

"Do I have to decide right now?"

"Of course not, dear. You've got a few days until I go. We can talk about it more tomorrow."

Nandara smiled but it didn't reach her eyes. Nandara folded Spark into her arms and hugged her so tightly Spark thought she might try to carry her off with her to the Red Mountains. She embraced Nanny for even longer.

"I won't keep you. Give Bren my wishes."

Then the crowds on the streets swallowed Nandara, and Nanny continued walking out into the plains, Spark trailing her. They passed by one of the smoke-belching mills on the edge of the city, and Spark glared at it the whole way. The mills were a new addition, sprung up like squat ugly toadstools, a blight on the farmland in the valley. Spark always wanted to blast the fires out of those great furnaces and bring the buildings to ruin. She couldn't account for why. Nanny hated them too. It was in the way her jaw tightened when they went by. But eventually, Nanny slumped, her head bowed and gaze focused on the ground ahead of them.

Spark couldn't stop watching her grandmother. She couldn't remember ever seeing her so sad, not even when people brought up Neesha, the thing that upset her most. It wasn't only the loss of her daughter that upset Nanny so much, but the loss of the dragons that followed so swiftly afterward. They were still out in the mountains but didn't come anywhere near Pasdale anymore, not when so many of them had been captured and forced into the mills.

Spark's attention was divided between concern for Nanny and trying to work out how she would finish her studies with Nandara and still find time to get the forge ready to make swords with Bren. She didn't think she could do anything to make Nanny feel better since the dragons couldn't be helped. And it was safer not to let her thoughts stray down that path. She had her family and that had to be enough. They had a birthday party to prepare for.

ACKNOWLEDGEMENTS

After nine years since my last novel came out, it's weird to release something new. Weird and exciting. It's taken time and patience, trial and error, to get my craft to where it is and have this book ready for publication.

It's weird to think of a book as a team effort, but this book wouldn't exist without some cheerleaders and coaches. Special thanks to my spouse and kiddo for all their support.

Thank you to Write Club, the KW Writers Alliance, and my Potted Plant folks for companionship through the pandemic, emotional support, and helping me push my craft and grow as a writer. A shout out to Kris for being loremaster of my little dragon world. Thanks to Una for making the words prettier and a little easier to understand.

And a big special thank you to everyone who backed or shared the Fireborn Kickstarter. This series couldn't have happened without your support!

ABOUT THE AUTHOR

photo by Mike Thode

Vanessa is a word sorceress and Nebula Award-winning fantasy author whose life seldom strays from the world of books, especially during winter hibernation. Even her volunteer work revolves around the literary world, currently as co-founder and events director of KW Writers Alliance and as coordinator for the SFWA volunteer team.

When she's not being bookish, she's into astronomy, hiking, gardening, and has a personal goal to visit all the national parks. Don't ask her about her love of trees unless you've got some time. She loves Halloween and hates to be cold. Vanessa lives in Waterloo (no, the other one) with her spouse, daughter, and dogs, where she can be found in her butterfly garden, achieving her final form as a garden witch.

To learn more, visit thodestool.ca or follow her on social media @VRicciThode